ALL NIGHT LONG

J. KENNER

All Night Long

by

J. Kenner

Chapter One

"VERDICT?" Selma Herrington asked as she tilted her head to better display her newest tattoo to Elena Anderson. A recent addition to the waitstaff at The Fix on Sixth, Elena also happened to be the owner's daughter. More importantly, over the last few months, Selma and Elena had bonded over a mutual love of whiskey, flea markets, and romance novels.

At ten in the morning, The Fix hadn't yet opened, and it was just the two of them in the cavernous bar. Later, at lunchtime, the place would start to fill, and when the evening rolled around, it would be jam-packed with all the customers who'd come to watch this week's Man of the Month contest for Mr. August. Selma knew that Elena's father, Tyree, and his three partners had started the contest as a way to draw interest to the bar and increase revenue. And though Selma didn't know the details, considering how packed the bar was on alternate Wednesdays—and how many new faces she saw every time she walked through the doors—she was certain the plan was working spectacularly.

So far, she'd only seen two of the Man of the Month contests, but she was determined to come tonight because she'd heard from her brother Matthew that one of their high school friends, Landon Ware, was entered. A cop, Landon didn't seem the type to reveal his abs on a stage, and Selma couldn't help but wonder if something else was going on. Recently, when she'd been in the back talking to Tyree about his order for two more cases of bourbon, she'd noticed Landon with Taylor, a regular who also acted as the show's stage manager. Maybe she'd find a moment to catch up with him before tonight's contest.

Right now, Selma stood at the long, polished oak bar beside Elena, who was rolling silverware into napkins. She added another roll to the pile, then focused more intently on Selma's shoulder. "Oh, that's nice," she said, her voice rich with genuine approval. She used a finger to pull the strap of Selma's black *Free-Tail Bat Bourbon* logo tank top to the side to better reveal the pattern of retro-style starbursts that exploded over Selma's pale skin. "This is what? Your seventh tat? When did you get it done?"

"Eighth," Selma said, running her fingers through her dark, choppy-cut hair that she'd recently tipped with cobalt blue. "And a couple of days ago."

"Catalyst?" Elena asked with an impish grin, her chocolate-brown eyes dancing with merriment. A tall black woman with pixie-style hair, perfect skin, and high cheekbones, Elena was stunning enough to be a model. And, in fact, Selma was trying to convince Elena to do a photo shoot for Selma, so that she could use the images in an upcoming Bat Bourbon ad campaign geared toward women.

Or she *had been* trying to convince Elena. Since Selma was on the verge of selling Austin Free-Tail Distillery so that she could dive into other adventures, the challenge of advertising her small-batch whiskeys was soon going to be someone else's problem.

Still, Elena would look damn good on a billboard fronting IH-35.

"Selma?"

Frowning, Selma pushed the random thoughts from her head. "Sorry. Mind wandering. What were you asking me?"

"What prompted the starburst tats?" Considering the relatively short time they'd known each other, Selma and Elena had grown incredibly close—at least by Selma's regimented definition of closeness. Close enough that Selma had confided that all her tats had been impulse ink—though Selma had never gone far enough to share the impetus behind those impulses. Not a single one was planned, and as far as Selma was concerned, none ever would be.

"I was poking around in Room Service," she told Elena now, referring to her favorite eclectic thrift store. "And I saw the pattern on some vintage dishes. I liked it, so I popped into True Blue Tattoo on Airport Boulevard and had it done on the way home."

She didn't mention that she'd bought the dishes, too. Nor did she mention that seeing them had sent little stabs straight into her heart. She didn't recall much about her early years, but she did remember eating grilled cheese sandwiches with her brother off of her grandmother's starburst pattern plates.

The memory had been lost until the moment she'd seen the dishes, and then it had all rushed back. The smell of the bread in the pan, the sizzle of cheese melting against the hot skillet as it drizzled from the edges. The way her grandmother hummed "My Darling Clementine" as she cooked. Matthew's incessant, stupid knock-knock jokes.

Those rare glimpses into a lost past were too precious to lose. And so Selma had done what Selma always did; she'd made a memory. This time, by marking it on her shoulder so that her grandmother would always be with her.

Elena, of course, knew none of that. Mostly because Selma had never even told her friend that she was adopted, much less that her birth mother had abandoned her ten-year-old daughter and eleven-year-old son in Lakeline Mall with nothing but a pair of matching backpacks with notes pinned to them.

No way would she share that. There were limits,

after all. And getting too close only made things complicated. And painful.

"Is that why you popped in this morning? To show me?" Elena pushed the pile of napkins closer to Selma. "Or did you come to help?"

"Actually, I came to talk to your dad."

"Checking stock?"

"Partly." Selma had founded Austin Free-Tail Distillery on a wing and a prayer just over five years ago, and it had grown into a small batch distillery with a nationwide reputation. Named in honor of Austin's famous colony of Mexican Free-tail bats, the distillery's various small batch varieties included Bat Bourbon and Dusk Flight Rye.

Before Free-Tail had exploded onto the scene, though, The Fix and its owner, Tyree Johnson, had been consistently loyal and supportive, going so far as to host a tasting event for her and the company long before anyone in Austin—or the country—had a clue who she was.

"To be honest," Selma told Elena as she helped roll the silverware, "I wanted to tell him my news and ask his advice."

"News? Did Free-Tail win another award?"

"No, but thanks for the vote of confidence."

"Now I'm dying of curiosity. Hang on." She walked the length of the bar to the small section that opened. She didn't bother with that, though, just slipped under, then pulled down two highball glasses and held them up to Selma. "I have a plan to ply you with alcohol so you'll tell me before you tell my dad. Too early for bourbon?"

"Ply away. And you know how I pay my bills these days. As far as I'm concerned, it's never too early for bourbon."

Elena put a golf ball sized ice cube in each glass then poured them both a pre-lunch appropriate shot. Instead of sliding the glasses across the bar to Selma, though, she held onto them as she slipped back under the bar, then headed for one of the two-tops. She plunked the glasses down, then dropped into a seat. "Okay. Tell."

As a rule, Selma wasn't one for obeying orders, but she'd been wanting to share with Elena for days, and she'd been hoping that her friend would be at the bar this morning. "Well, the truth is, I'm moving to Scotland."

Elena had just lifted her glass, but now she put it back down without taking a sip. "You're what?"

Selma tilted her head and eyed her friend. There wasn't a thing wrong with Elena's hearing.

"Wow," Elena said, and now she really did take a sip. "When did this come about? Have you thought it all through? How are you going to run the distillery?"

Selma bristled, and for a second, she considered backing away from the topic altogether. But she knew Elena didn't mean anything bad, even if she did sound a little too much like Selma's adoptive mother. And for years Allison Herrington had been insisting that Selma was the best little girl in the world. Or, rather, she would be if she'd stop being so damned impulsive.

"Of course I've thought it through. I have a temporary gig lined up over there, and after that's done, I can use the cash to fund about a year of traveling around Europe. Maybe even tag on Asia or Australia."

"Yeah, but Scotland? Who's going to run Free-Tail? And where is this all coming from? I mean, it's one thing to decide to drive to Montana for a concert."

Something Selma had recently done, to Elena's amusement. "But it's another thing altogether to up and move to another country."

Selma just shrugged. Her friend wasn't wrong. But Selma liked to keep moving. She wanted adventure. New scenery. And since it wasn't going to come to her, she had to go to it.

"How did this come about?" Elena asked.

"Do you remember me telling you about Sean O'Reilly?"

"Is he the one you met when you flew off to back-pack around Scotland after college?"

"The same. Although it was more *during* college. Or, technically, it was after I dropped out."

Elena leaned back with an amused expression. "And? How does he fit into the picture now?"

"I'm going over to Scotland to work in a couple of his distilleries." She'd met Sean more than a decade ago after she'd left college life behind. She'd been making A's in all her classes, but the whole learn-shit-through-books thing really hadn't jelled with her. So she'd decided that rather than learn about Lord Byron and Robert Burns and Robert Louis

Stevenson and so many other Scottish poets from some grad student standing in for a professor in Austin, she'd fly to the source and learn as much as she could on her own.

She'd formally dropped out on a Friday, and the following Monday she boarded a plane with a backpack, a phone, a credit card, and absolutely no agenda whatsoever. It had been heaven. She'd explored the cities and towns, she'd talked to locals, she'd read poetry on a bench in Edinburgh Castle. She'd crashed in hostels and made friends with other students.

Best of all, she'd met Sean. He'd lent her twenty pounds when her credit card had been declined, and when she'd paid him back the following day, he'd used the money to buy her a variety of Scotch whiskies for her to taste. She'd known a bit about spirits—she'd played around with distilling in college—but back then she'd mostly been a wine girl. But with Sean, she'd discovered not only a taste for Scotch, but that she had an excellent palate. So good, in fact, that Sean had offered her a summer job in his distillery in the Highlands.

She'd taken it, on the condition that he understood it wasn't permanent. She'd come to Scotland to explore, and that's what she'd intended to do. But she hadn't been averse to taking a job to fund a few further adventures.

She'd ended up in his bed with the same caveats. Her trip to the Highlands was all about fun, and a good time was all she'd been looking for.

After two months, she'd learned more than she ever expected about Scotch and quite a bit more about having fun in bed.

Elena's brow furrowed. "So, is there something going on between you two?"

"Definitely no." Back in the day, Sean O'Reilly's thick Scottish brogue had tickled her senses, making her think of hot men in kilts and the seductive historical romances that had helped her survive those horrible years before Mom and Dad had adopted her and Matthew. They'd shared good times in bed and an interest in fine whisky, but that had been all. He'd been her tasty morsel years ago, but Selma made it a point to never look back. Why would she when the world was filled with such a variety of delicious opportunities?

"Does *he* know that?"

Selma laughed. "Duh. Have you ever known me to be coy? Besides, he told me he's engaged to a local girl. But he assures me that I won't lack for hunky Scottish companionship."

Elena rolled her eyes. "Highlanders and what's under their kilts aside, why on earth are you going all the way to Scotland to work in a distillery when you own an up-and-coming one right here?"

"Well, yeah, that's kind of the rest of it. I'm selling Free-Tail."

Elena almost knocked over her glass. "You're *selling* Free-Tail? Now? You're on the brink of breaking out. Restaurants in over a dozen states stock your bourbon. Why on earth would you do that?"

"Exactly my question."

The deep voice came from the opposite side of the cavernous bar, and Selma twisted in her chair to see Tyree Johnson eating up the floor as he crossed to them in long, measured strides. A tall man with a shaved head, a neatly trimmed beard, and skin as dark as Elena's, Tyree seemed to fill the room. His broad chest and shoulders would have been intimidating were it not for the genuine kindness that seemed to roll off him.

"Tell me I'm hearing things."

"You're not," she said firmly. "This is the best decision. *My* decision."

She watched as his eyes met Elena's. For two people who hadn't even met until a few months ago, they shared a lot of the same mannerisms, not to mention similar features. But what made Selma smile as the two shared a glance was the deep affection she saw in Tyree's eyes. This time last year, he hadn't even known he had a daughter. Now, just the expression on his face revealed how much he adored her. Not to mention Elena's mother, Eva, with whom he'd fallen in love all over again after a separation of more than twenty years.

If she weren't so flustered about both their negative reactions to her new life plan, Selma would actually be feeling a little gooey at the moment.

As it was, she felt on pins and needles. Like she had to justify her decisions. Which, of course, she didn't. But apparently she was going to anyway, because she tapped the table top for their attention. "Hey," she said when they looked at her. "Don't bring me down, okay? I know what I'm doing, and I'm ecstatic about this offer. I'm going to make a ton of money on the sale, the brand I built will live on, and I'll have the freedom to do cool things. Like go work for a few months in Scotland. Then maybe work in a winery in France. Or take painting lessons. Or learn to sail in Monaco and practice my French in Nice. The whole world becomes my playground. How is that a bad thing?"

For a moment, Tyree said nothing. Then he pulled a chair over from a nearby two-top. As he sat, he rested his hand on hers, his big palm completely covering her smaller one. "It's not," he said. "And I'm glad to hear that you've thought this out."

"I have," she said, probably a little defensively. "I never expected Free-Tail to grow so big so fast. I'd always assumed I'd have the freedom to walk away for a few months, take long vacations, all that kind of thing."

Tyree nodded slowly. "Makes sense. At the same time, it's a testament to your talent that it has grown so fast. You've built the distillery into something to be proud of."

"And I am proud of it. Just like you're proud of The Fix." She looked around the bar, with its rustic Texas interior. The cavernous main room that played host to dozens of strategically placed tables. The long bar and the wall of glass shelves that displayed an array of sparkling bottles filled with liquor, including bottles from her own distillery.

Tyree had renovated the property and opened The Fix on Sixth about six years ago, and the place was really turning into an Austin staple. Selma knew it had been touch and go for a while, but now that the bar was running a bi-weekly calendar guy contest, she was pretty sure they were firmly in the black. She hoped so; she loved the bar and would hate to see it close its doors.

And to be brutally honest, once she sold her distillery and moved to Scotland, Selma knew she'd miss this place. But that didn't mean she wanted to be locked to it anymore than she wanted to be locked to her own business.

"You did an amazing thing here," she told Tyree. "You wanted to save this place so badly, and you managed to pull it off in a big way." Recently, the bar had run into financial trouble. The calendar contest had been part of an overall plan to turn the bar's financials around.

"We're not quite there yet," he said. "But I think we're on track."

"I'm sure you are," Selma said. "And after fighting so hard for what you built, I can see why you think I'm nuts. But I'm not ready to settle down yet. Not with a man or a career." She lifted a shoulder. "I'm a leaf on the wind, and I want to see where the breeze takes me next. Besides," she added with a smug smile, "the offer is from a huge publicly traded company that owns a lot of labels. They're going to keep my brand alive and pay me really well."

For a second, she thought Tyree might argue, but then he nodded. "Fair enough."

"Does that mean you'll help me?"

His mouth curved down into a frown. "Not sure how I'm supposed to do that," he said. "But if I can, I will."

"That's why I came here this morning. I need to find an attorney to handle the sale of the distillery. And everyone I've talked to suggests the same man. I wanted to find out who you'd recommend."

"Well, I'm not sure who you're being referred to, but if it were me, I'd talk to Easton Wallace."

Selma's cheeks almost cracked from the force of maintaining her smile. "Actually, he seems to be the perennial favorite. I've heard rumors he's going to run for election in the next judicial race. Considering how popular he is, I'm guessing he's going to win."

Across the table, Elena leaned forward. "But he's not popular with you?"

"Oh, no, it's not that. Easton's great." She felt the warmth creep up the back of her neck and hoped that she wasn't turning red. Since she so rarely blushed, the possibility was especially mortifying. "It's just that we knew each other back when he was in law school. And I know that he works out at Matthew's gym," she added, referring to her brother and the local gym he owned. "And I figure it might be simpler to have an attorney you don't know in real life. I mean, I'm opinionated. What if he doesn't agree with the deal points I want to raise?"

That was a legitimate concern, but she was more afraid of not being able to pay proper attention to the legal issues. Selma had a strict no-return policy with men. But she'd walked away from Easton far too early in the game. She knew that because even after all these years she hadn't forgotten him. Not him or all the wicked things he'd done to her body on their one night together.

Tyree waved her concerns away—or, rather, he waved her concerns about legal disagreements away. "Not an issue. Easton's as professional as they come. He'll tell you his opinion, but he'll also fight for the deal you want so long as it's legitimate and legal. I've hired him for a number of things. Trust me, he's the man you want."

That, of course, was the trouble. She still wanted Easton. She'd been left with a perpetual itch that needed scratching. An itch that was surely the by-product of her too-hasty departure. But still persistent enough that she was tempted to break her own rules.

Because when you got right down to it, if she was about to haul herself all the way to Scotland, then maybe—just maybe—she owed herself one hell of a send-off.

Chapter Two

"TEN DAYS. TWO WEEKS MAXIMUM." Fifth Circuit Court of Appeals Judge Desmond Coale stroked his gray-streaked beard as his deep gray eyes—still sharp despite his eighty-plus years—focused intently on Easton. "Anyone who's paying attention knows you're planning to run, but we still want to be deliberate with the timing of your formal announcement. There's an advantage to being first out of the gate. We both know that."

"We do," Easton agreed, feeling a bit like the twenty-four-year-old law grad he used to be, and not the thirty-five-year-old accomplished attorney he'd grown into. Accomplished enough, in fact, that he now occupied a corner office in one of the most prestigious firms in Texas, if not the country. And though he wasn't yet a partner, that wasn't for lack of skill or invitation. Instead, he was remaining a salaried employee so that he would have no formal ties to any particular firm when he officially threw his hat into the ring for the Travis County District Court judicial election.

At the moment he was standing in front of his coveted floor-to-ceiling corner windows looking down Congress Avenue toward the Texas State Capital building. Who knew? Maybe one day he'd be seated there during a legislative session. Certainly, if Judge Coale had his way, Easton would. And his mentor hadn't steered him wrong yet.

He turned away from the window and looked at his friend, mentor, and former boss. The judge was seated in one of the leather guest chairs that faced Easton's massive desk, the top of which was completely clear except for a single yellow legal pad. As far as Easton was concerned, a cluttered desk meant a cluttered mind, not to mention a scattershot lifestyle. And he prided himself on being sharp and laser-focused.

The judge pushed his half-rim glasses up his nose. "If we both agree on the value of being the first to announce, then do you want to tell me why you're still mucking around?"

Easton almost laughed. That was one of the reasons Judge Coale had made a reputation for himself as a federal appellate court judge—the man didn't pull his punches. And that was one of the reasons that Easton considered the older man both a friend and a pseudo grandparent.

"I didn't realize I was."

"Don't bullshit me, son. You've grown into a damn fine poker player, but I'm still a better one."

"That you are, sir," Easton said, hiding his grin.

"This is what we've been working toward since the first day you stepped into my office, all puffed up and ready to save the world one trial at a time."

"No argument. Except possibly about the puffed-up part."

The judge chuckled. "Twenty-four years old and certain you were God's gift to jurisprudence. And, honestly, you may have been right. You're one of the most talented young lawyers I've run across. And those first couple of years in the district attorney's office were a smart move. But I'm glad you've become more strategic about your practice. If your path is going to take you to where I'm sitting—and let's be clear, I think you have what it takes to be a Federal judge—then who you know is at least as important as your legal mind. You can't get appointed if you're not noticed."

"Agreed. And the first step is to sit on a local bench." Easton had made up his mind to be an attorney when he was thirteen years old and watched as his blue-collar parents had lost everything—including their house—because a major corporation stepped in to request eminent domain over a crappy section of land on the outskirts of his small northeastern hometown.

Despite the fact that a state's power of eminent domain shouldn't—and technically didn't—extend to forcibly buying property for the use of a business entity, the deal went through. The government bought the land, then rented it to the corporation.

His parents—who had a long-term lease on a section of the property from where they operated a popular hamburger stand—were tossed off with no recourse. They'd lost everything following that debacle, including the house Easton had grown up in, and it had taken the rest of their adult lives to recover.

That's when Easton had decided that he'd become a lawyer no matter what the cost. He'd pursued a clerkship with a Federal judge with relentless energy, knowing that the connections and skills—not to mention the prestige of the position—would only help him in the future. After his two-year stint with Judge Coale, he'd aimed his attention toward criminal law, knowing he could get the best education as a trial lawyer in the fast-paced criminal world. He'd moved next to the prestigious mid-size firm where he now worked so that he would have exposure to several sub-practices of law. His ultimate goal had been to open his own firm and specialize in plaintiff's work, helping people like his parents who'd stood in the shoes of David while facing a corporate Goliath. And Easton would stand in as the stone with which David toppled the giant.

The way had been paved since he was thirteen and he'd dutifully walked the path until he met Judge

Coale. The judge had invited him to dinner about two years ago and planted the seeds of the judiciary. It hadn't been something Easton had initially considered, but there was no doubt that a judge had influence, both on and off the bench. And what better way to help people like his parents than to be the arbiter on their final battlefield?

So he'd accepted the judge's proposition. Judge Coale would make sure Easton knew all the right people and the right steps toward securing a seat on the bench. And the judge knew his stuff. He'd started his career as an elected probate judge, then stair-stepped his way up to serve many years as an elected justice on the Texas Supreme Court before receiving a presidential appointment to the Federal Fifth Circuit Court of Appeals. With those kinds of credentials, Easton figured he couldn't have found a better mentor.

Currently, Easton was planning to make a bid for a new district court seat in Travis County that had been established in the last legislative session. Since the seat was new, he didn't have to challenge an incumbent, and so far his drip campaign was working well. He'd garnered a lot of support among key players in the city, both in and outside the legal community.

Now he just had to keep up the momentum.

"What's on your agenda the rest of this week and next?" the judge asked. "Let's get you seen everywhere for the ten or so days, then waltz into the county clerk's office and formally announce a week from next Tuesday. We can put a bug in the ear of a few reporters so that *The Austin Chronicle* and *The Austin American Statesman* both run a story."

"And the *Daily Texan*," Easton said, referring to the University of Texas's daily newspaper. "Don't forget the importance of the new voters. Especially since I'm a UT law grad."

"I like the way you think."

"You should. You trained me."

The intercom on Easton's phone buzzed, and a moment later the thirtieth-floor receptionist's voice filtered over the line. "There's a woman here to see you," Sandra said. "Says she's an old friend and has a contractual issue to discuss."

"Did she give you her name?"

"Jean," Sandy said. "Jean Rockwell."

Easton glanced at the judge, then shrugged. "The name doesn't ring a bell. But tell her I'm in a meeting but will be out to see her in a minute."

She promised to do that, then the line went dead.

"I should probably get back to work," Easton told the judge. "I appreciate the lunch, though." He glanced over at the remains of the Franklin Barbecue take-out that still littered the top of his small conference table. The popular East Austin barbecue joint with its insane lines had become a destination for celebrities and politicians, with everyone from President Obama to Kanye West visiting the place. How Judge Coale had managed to get take-out without waiting for six hours was anyone's guess.

"We'll talk soon," the judge said, rising. "Your week is full?"

"Tomorrow morning I'm in Dallas for depositions, then at a fundraiser for the Austin Opera in the evening. Friday I have dinner with Senator Todd. And Saturday evening I'll be speaking at the literacy benefit at the Exotic Game Ranch."

"And Sunday?"

"Drinks with a friend," Easton said, then held up his hand. "He owns a gym and knows pretty much everyone in town. I'm not going to specifically ask him to chat me up, but he's a good enough friend that he will without asking."

"Then by all means, don't ditch him."

Easton tapped his nose. "Exactly."

"And tonight?"

"Booked," he said.

The judge nodded. "Deposition prep, of course."

That wasn't Easton's plan, but he didn't bother to correct his mentor. Somehow, Easton doubted that the judge would find attending this week's Man of the Month contest at The Fix on Sixth to be an appropriate candidate event. But his friend and client, Tyree Johnson owned the bar, and Easton was friends with a number of the bar's employees and regulars. Including Detective Landon Ware and Taylor D'Angelo, the woman Landon was protecting. Considering Easton was the one who suggested that Landon enter the contest as bait to flush out

Taylor's stalker, Easton thought he ought to at least make an appearance.

He'd even seen Selma Herrington there a few times, and hadn't that been a punch in the gut? More than ten years had passed, but sometimes as he was falling asleep, he still trembled from the memory of the way her skin felt as her body slid over his, not to mention the magical things she'd done with that wide, hot mouth.

The judge slipped on his blue seersucker jacket. "And who's accompanying you to the fundraiser and the benefit?"

Easton cleared his throat, wishing the act would clear out the memories that were making him uncomfortably hard. And wouldn't a woman like Selma be interesting—and dangerous—on his arm?

That, however, wouldn't happen. For one, Easton wasn't stupid. He knew that playing it safe meant playing to win. And Easton never did anything if it wasn't with the goal of winning.

For another, Selma had disappeared on him after one of the most amazing nights he'd ever shared with a woman. A small fact that had pissed him off at the time.

He was over it now. But definitely not inclined to track her down and ask her out again just to end up rejected. In that direction lay madness. "Actually, I was planning on going stag." Easton kept his voice level. He and the judge had been over this ground before.

"I'm not suggesting that wedding bells need to start ringing, but taking a date gives you a—what do they call it?—a wingman. Someone starts asking you incendiary questions, she can subtly change the subject. You get trapped, she can signal to you from across the room. Trust me, son, a competent date can be one of your best election tools. And who knows where it might lead? Look at Deborah and me."

The judge and his wife had met when the senator who'd mentored Judge Coale had suggested that his own daughter accompany him to various charitable and local functions. And, Easton had to admit, they were the perfect couple.

Easton, however, saw no one similarly appropriate on his personal horizon, as he'd told the judge several times.

"Take Marianne," the judge stated, referring to

another lawyer in the firm, and clearly expecting the order to be followed. "You need someone who's presentable and well-spoken. Someone who can hold her own in a conversation and knows how to avoid the quicksand of certain politically charged topics."

"Yes, but Marianne is—"

"She's perfect, son. And don't tell me you're not interested in her. That's not the point. This is a game, as you well know. Hell, as *she* well knows. She won't be expecting matrimony. She's savvy enough to realize that being your regular date means she'll have a chip to call in later with you."

"I don't—"

Judge Coale held up his hands. "I can't tell you what to do, son. I can only tell you what you *should* do. It's your choice whether you play the game right or not."

Easton managed not to crack a smile. "Subtle."

"I do my best." The judge pulled open the door. "Now I'm going to go see what Jordan's up to," he said, referring to the firm's senior partner.

"As always, it's been a pleasure."

"We'll talk soon," the judge said, then turned to walk down the hall as if he owned it while Easton went the opposite direction toward reception.

He pushed through the doors with a nod toward Sandy. Mostly, however, his attention had been captured by the woman in the tight black jeans and waist-skimming blouse. She was facing away from him, which was a good thing since he found himself mesmerized. She had long, lean legs, a heart shaped ass that his hands itched to palm, and short blue-tipped hair that looked so silky he could almost imagine the feel of it against his skin.

But it was when she bent forward to take a magazine off the table that his heart almost stopped. Her blouse rose, revealing her lower back in the process —along with an intricate tattoo of chain link dotted by individual roses. Some blooming. Some buds. Some dying on the vine.

His skin heated. And he was suddenly in desperate need of a glass of water.

He knew that tattoo.

Like hell this woman was Jean Rockwell. As if he'd spoken aloud, she turned around, and he found himself looking into the cunning green eyes of Selma Herrington.

"Hello, Easton." Her voice, husky and sensual and dangerously familiar, rolled over him, and he felt his cock go hard as effectively as the most potent aphrodisiac. "It's been a very long time."

Chapter Three

NEVER HAD Easton been so happy that he'd appeared in so many courtrooms in front of so many judges in so many different situations. Not only did those hours upon hours give him the experience to make him into the lawyer he was today, but they also helped him to develop an almost perfect poker face.

And that was an asset that came in pretty damn handy at the moment.

"Ms. Rockwell," he said, extending his hand. "I'm so glad you left your name. I don't think I would have recognized you."

"Really?" Selma was the kind of person whose bright smile was almost radioactive. She flashed that wide grin now, and for a moment he simply basked in its warmth. "Because you don't seem to have changed at all." Her gaze roamed over him, so slow and deliberate he had to fight the urge to pull her close and dare her to use her hands instead of her eyes.

She paused her inspection at his crotch, and he almost lost it when her teeth dragged over her lower lip before she lifted her face to his, her gaze positively smoldering. "I take it back," she said. "You're still the same. Only better."

Oh, holy hell. All he could think was that he was damn glad that his back was to Sandy and that he was blocking the receptionist's view.

That, and the pressing urgency of getting her out of the reception area before he said or did something stupid. He'd forgotten how hard it was to behave normally around Selma Herrington. Probably because all the blood in his head had raced to more southern regions.

He cleared his throat and forced himself to be professional. He also took a step back. "It's wonderful to see you again, but I'm sorry to say I'm not taking on any new clients. I'd be happy to walk you down, though, and we can catch up on the way."

"Or maybe we could chat in your office, and you can recommend someone else? I've got a time-sensitive deal brewing." She tilted her head, her eyes narrowing a bit as if she was taking his measure. "Unless you can't handle the pressure?" Her lips pressed together, and he was certain she was holding back laughter. "Of recommending someone to replace you, I mean."

"Ms. Rockwell, I assure you. No one can replace me." It was his turn to smile. "But I can help you find second best."

He nodded to Sandy, who thankfully seemed oblivious, then led Selma down the hall and into his office, shutting the door behind him

"A corner office." She walked to the window behind his desk, stepping casually into what he considered his personal space. "And with one hell of a view." She turned to face him. "You really have come up in the world."

He moved closer, intentionally encroaching on *her* personal space. Selma, however, didn't seem to mind. "I've worked hard," he said. "It's paid off."

He crossed the room until he stopped right in front of her. So close he could smell a hint of vanilla, and the visceral memories the scent inspired almost had him thrusting her back against the window and crushing his mouth to hers.

Thankfully, he had more self-control than that. Instead, he said, "I may have a corner office, but you're not doing too badly yourself. I've read about Free-Tail. That's quite a business you've built."

"It is." She started to take a step backwards, as if she was uncomfortable, but there was no place to go. She was mere inches from the wall of glass overlooking downtown Austin.

Easton wondered briefly if her discomfort was because of his proximity or the mention of her distillery, but right then he didn't need an answer. He pressed on. "I've seen you around a few times since our night. But it's only been in recent years. At The Fix. Once on Congress Avenue. One time at Herrington's Gym. But never back then. I didn't catch one glimpse of you for years after that night."

Before, they'd spent almost three consecutive nights chatting and flirting in a local bar that had gone out of business years ago. But then he'd offered to drive her to where she was housesitting, and they'd ended up naked on the couch, never even making it to the bedroom until almost dawn, when they both got a spectacular second wind.

And then she'd ghosted him.

"Somehow, you managed to disappear from my world without a trace. Handy trick."

"Not really a trick," she said lightly. "After all, I bet you didn't try too hard to find me. A hot shot law student who went on to be an assistant district attorney and then a powerful lawyer. I bet even back then you had access to a slew of investigators. If you'd wanted to, you'd have found someone to turn over the right rock. But you're a man who had other things on your mind." She met his eyes defiantly, and he had to admit she'd earned points. He'd been watching her face. Looking for regret. For guilt. He saw only a woman as tough and polished and unreadable as himself.

She was right, too. He hadn't looked hard. He'd regretted it when he realized that she'd meant what she said about no second date. No more casual get-togethers. But he'd been determined to graduate at the top of his law school class. Sex was the last thing on his mind. And, honestly, if Selma had been around, sex might have been hard to ignore.

"Probably true," he admitted. "And I have to admit, it was easier to study with no distractions."

"Was I a distraction?"

He took one more step toward her. "I think you know the answer to that. We knew each other for what? Thirty-six hours? You were the wildest, fastest, hottest time in bed I'd ever had. And then you pulled the plug and walked away."

She tilted her head, and when she spoke, her voice was breathy. "Sounds like you still want me."

Hell, yeah, he did. But all he said was, "I'm not the man I was back then."

"No?" She leaned closer, and he could feel her heat. He remembered that about her. How her skin had burned against his. Selma Herrington ran hot as a furnace, the walking definition of a hot-blooded woman. "Then why don't you tell me what kind of a man you are now?"

He took a deliberate step back. "One who knows the distinction between want and willpower. Right now, the only thing I want is to know why you walked away."

"And the only thing I want is your help." Her smile was flirty. "I wonder if we'll both get our heart's desire."

He studied her, but there were no clues to who she was now or what she was doing there. If he wanted more, he was going to have to ask. "All right. You can tell me why you're here. I'm not promising I'll help, but I'll hear you out."

"Thank—"

"But on one condition."

"I don't do conditions."

"Then we're at an impasse."

She looked at him, apparently decided he meant it, and shrugged. "What's your condition?"

"I just told you. I want to know why you walked away."

The tilt of her head was almost imperceptible. "I'm surprised, counselor. I didn't think it was wise for a lawyer to reveal too much of himself."

"Like I said, the man you slept with doesn't exist anymore. But that doesn't mean the man who remains isn't still curious."

"I tell you, you help me?"

"I said I'd hear you out," he clarified. "That was the deal."

This time when her lips pressed together, there was nothing flirty or contrived about it. She was thinking. Finally, she spoke. "Honestly? I liked you too much."

That wasn't what he was expecting to hear. "What?"

"You heard me."

"What the hell does that mean?"

"Exactly what it sounds like."

"Why would you have to leave because you liked me too much?"

Now, she laughed. "Sorry, counselor. Quid pro quo, remember? I gave you quid, now I want my quo."

He considered arguing, but he'd set the rules. She was only playing by them. "Fair enough," he said as he took a seat behind his desk, then gestured for her to sit in a guest chair.

She hesitated, then complied. "I've had an offer to buy my distillery. A very nice offer," she added, and when she told him the number, he whistled. "I'd like you to negotiate the deal for me."

"Why me?"

"I want the best. Your name keeps popping up."

"I'm flattered, but I'll be honest. If that's their initial offer, you don't need the best. You just need someone competent. Because that company wants your brand, and they're willing to give you pretty much anything you ask for to get it."

"Maybe. But I don't like to do things half-assed. When I'm in, I'm all in."

"Bullshit."

Her eyes went wide, and even Easton was surprised that he'd said it. "Excuse me?"

Shit. He debated what to say, then decided to be all in himself. "You and I were half-assed."

Her mouth quirked into a sideways grin. "From your perspective, but from mine I was doing exactly what I wanted the way I wanted." She met his eyes. Held them. "Fast and hot and dirty. And don't think you were the only one. Sometimes for a night. Sometimes a week. Sometimes a month. Maybe you got the short straw, but I already told you why. Honestly, you should be flattered. But if you thought there was going to be more than a fast, fun time, then that was your misinterpretation. Not mine." She tilted her head. "But considering it's been over ten years, you seem kind of hung up on the subject."

She was right, dammit. From the moment he'd seen that familiar rose and chain-link tattoo, he'd felt the shift in the air. The awareness. Like the electricity that precedes a lightning storm. Only in this case, the storm was Selma. And if he wasn't careful, she'd sweep him away.

"Just trying to figure you out," he said, masking the real answer under a patina of truth. "I like puzzles. And you qualify. But going back to half-assed, I wasn't trying to analyze you and me. I was offering evidence in contradiction of your statement. You say you don't do anything half-assed, and yet you're walking away from Free-Tail just as it's on the rise."

"Yeah, well, think what you want, but you're

completely off-base." This time, the heat in her voice wasn't seductive.

"I touched a nerve. Sorry."

Immediately, her shoulders sagged. "Look, let's pretend like you just graduated law school. And your grades were stellar and you were nine kinds of hot shit and you could totally write your own ticket."

"Sounds good so far."

"But what if it didn't sound good to you?"

He tilted his head, homing in on the serious note in her voice. He had a feeling that for the first time, he was about to see a glimpse of the real Selma. About ten years after he stopped caring.

"I mean, what if you'd only gone to law school on a whim? What if you were good, but by the time you got out, you didn't really care? It wasn't what you wanted to do, and you knew it?"

He shifted in his chair, suddenly not so comfortable with the conversation. "That would be a damn shame."

"If you stayed—if you did it anyway—to my way

of thinking, *that's* half-assed. Because you're not being true to yourself. I'm selling now because the distillery isn't my thing."

"What is?"

She shrugged, then flashed a sunshine-filled smile. "I'm still trying to figure that out. And I intend to have a damn good time doing it."

As he considered her words, she stood up, then came around to lean against his desk. He lifted a brow, watching her, but didn't urge her away. Slowly, she eased to the middle, so that she was standing right in front of him, her rear pressed against his desk, and her breasts about eye level as he tilted back in the leather chair.

She wore bright blue stiletto slides with perfectly matched toenail polish, and now she lifted one foot and placed it on the edge of the seat, right between his thighs. There was no contact between them, but even so, his balls tightened. He looked up and their eyes locked. "A damn good time," she repeated.

"Is this what you're looking for?" He slid her foot free, then tossed the shoe to the ground. Slowly, he moved her bare foot to the crotch of his designer slacks. "Negotiations with your buyer during the day? And more intimate negotiations with me at night?"

"Would that be so terrible?"

"You walked away from me once. Why come back now?"

"Same answer." She curled her toes, and he almost came right then. "I like you." Her grin turned impish as she focused on his cock, now very evident under the silk blend material of his slacks. She raised a single eyebrow. "And I think you like me, too."

"Under the circumstances, I won't even try to deny it."

"Good." She flexed her foot, and it was all he could do not to rise up and push her back onto his desk. A few buttons and zippers, and he could be buried inside her in seconds. He couldn't deny he wanted it —hell, he practically craved it—and unless he was delusional, she wanted it, too.

If she'd walked into his office a few years ago, he wouldn't have hesitated. He would have locked the door and fucked her senseless on his desk, his conference table, against the floor-to-ceiling windows with the cityscape looming behind them. He would have spread her wide and buried his face between her legs, his hand over her mouth to muffle the sound of her moans.

But that was the Easton who spent his days working his ass off toward his goal of opening his own firm. And in those days, he'd been more than happy for a wild time to take the edge off.

Today's Easton, however, had to watch his back. And even if she was all about a repeat performance, a steady relationship, and a ring, a wild child like Selma was not the woman a judicial candidate needed to have in his bed. Or on his arm.

Gently, he eased her foot away. "I do like you," he repeated. "But like isn't the issue." He pushed back his chair and stood, not meeting her surprised, wide eyes. "I'm sorry," he said. "I'm just not taking new clients right now."

Chapter Four

WITH ONLY FIFTEEN minutes to the start of the Man of the Month contest for Mr. April, the noise level in The Fix on Sixth had reached almost epic proportions. So loud, in fact, that in order to be heard, Selma had to lean sideways and practically yell into her brother's ear.

"Do you have any idea what possessed Landon to strut across the stage?" Their friend, Detective Landon Ware, was currently in the smaller back bar that served as a staging area during the bi-weekly Man of the Month contests. Soon, though, the emcee would call his name and he'd stride down the red carpet and onto the stage, where he'd rip his shirt off, flex his muscles, and generally try to garner votes.

"It's really not like him," Selma said. "Has he told you what's up?"

"Not a word."

"Weird." She cast a sideways glance at Matthew, wondering if he was keeping Landon's secrets. Secrets were something they were both good at, but that was about where the similarities ended. Because where she'd gone a little wild after their birth mother ditched them, Matthew had played by the rules even more. That probably made sense. He'd always been an introvert. And Selma was about as extroverted as a person could get.

Still, she wished a little of her personality had rubbed off on her brother. Despite his naturally hot body that had been enhanced by gym ownership, Matthew hadn't had a steady girlfriend in ages. Not that he didn't attract female attention—he did. He never lacked for a date, though he rarely got serious, always claiming he was too busy working or training.

Maybe that was true, but Selma thought it went the other way, and that he worked and trained to avoid dating. A genuinely nice guy, he'd always been shy around women. And while he dated on and off, he'd never settled down. Neither had Selma, of course. But she had no intention of settling any time soon. Matthew, however, longed for a family. And she wished there was a way to hug some of her crazy vivaciousness into him.

Then again, he was probably sitting beside her wishing he had a way to pass off some of his calming influence to her.

"You're coming to the gym tomorrow morning, right?" he asked, his voice raised over the din.

"Are you buying me breakfast?"

"Sure."

"Then I'm there."

"Cool. I wanted to run something by you, and— hey, isn't that Easton? Did you talk to him about selling the distillery?"

She turned to follow the direction of his gaze, only to find her stomach curdling in what could only be jealousy when she saw his head bent close to Taylor's. She couldn't see his face, but she didn't need to. That chiseled face was etched in her mind. And there was no mistaking the thick, dark hair or those incredibly broad shoulders, strong enough to hold a woman tight.

What on earth were he and Taylor discussing so intently? Were they involved? Was that why he'd turned her down?

She was pondering that unpleasant possibility when Cam, the bartender, sidled up. With his sultry blue-gray eyes, it was no wonder he'd won the title of Mr. March. Now, though, he just wanted their orders.

"A shot of Bat Bourbon," Selma said, with absolutely no ego. It just happened that her bourbon was the best.

"You got it," Cam said. "And by the way, thanks for letting me buy that case at cost. Mina loves it," he added, referring to his girlfriend, who Selma had met once or twice.

"You're totally welcome," Selma said. "I figure a bartender who takes my bourbon home is a walking, talking advertisement."

"Pretty much. I rave about it. But I heard a rumor you're selling. Say it isn't so."

She scrunched up her face and shrugged. "It's so. Time for the next adventure."

"Well, hell." Cam waved at a customer a few seats down, signaling that he'd be right there. "I'd love to stock up on a few cases before somebody swoops in and ruins your brand."

A shot of alarm cut through Selma, but before she could respond, Cam had slid down the bar to pour a couple of martinis.

"Do you think he meant that?" she asked Matthew.

Her brother shrugged. "Once you sell, it's out of your hands. And you never answered my question. What did Easton say about the sale?"

"Oh. That." She took a sip of the bourbon that Cam had poured for her. "He turned me down cold."

"Was it because he's running for a judge seat? He hasn't announced officially, but I overhear a lot of conversation at the gym, and everyone expects him to run."

"I think that's it." The words came out sharper than she intended, and Matthew glanced sideways at her, his look more perceptive than was comfortable.

She shrugged. Whether he turned her down because he was too busy or because he didn't think it wise to be associated with a woman who didn't own a single Chanel suit, it all came down to the same thing. She didn't have an attorney, and the deal was coming up fast.

"You know what? I'm going to go talk to him again."

"You should. I heard he was doing some legal work for Taylor. Maybe if you ask him to reconsider while he's talking to her, it'll guilt him into it."

She almost laughed out loud. "I don't know, big brother. Keep that up, and people are going to think you've started taking after me."

"I assure you, I have a limited quota of deviousness. I think I've hit my max for the year."

With a final grin to her brother, she hopped off the stool, intending to head toward Easton. At the same time, she realized that the ball of hard, cold jealousy had begun to dissolve with the revelation that Easton was Taylor's attorney. "I just want to ask him one thing. But if I'm not back by the time Landon trots up onto the stage, take some pics for me."

With Matthew waving her away, she headed toward the front tables where Easton was sitting with Taylor. He turned toward her, his gorgeous eyes widening almost imperceptibly. And though he would have been justified to be irritated with her, all she saw in those eyes was the warmth of a pleasant surprise.

Even so, it was Taylor who spoke first, bursting out with a laugh followed by, "Bat girl!" She grinned. "Sorry, I couldn't resist. I started calling you that to myself when I first saw you delivering stock. I love your stuff."

"Thanks."

"Don't you have a delivery crew? I mean, you're getting to be pretty well-known now."

"I had to break down and hire some folks recently," she admitted. "But I like to do some of the deliveries myself. Keep my hand in it. Meet the customers."

"Is that so?" Easton had shifted his stance, so that now he was looking directly at her, his eyes full of speculation.

She shrugged, strangely uncomfortable with his

intense examination, then turned her attention back to Taylor. "I'll bring you a couple of bottles."

"Really? That would be great."

"Sure. Word of mouth is the best advertising."

"Thanks," Taylor said, grinning and looking like it was Christmas morning while Easton maintained that odd, pensive expression.

Selma frowned, debating whether to simply walk away. But now that she was here, she didn't want to squander the opportunity.

She cleared her throat. "Am I interrupting? Because I had one thing to add to that legal matter we were talking about earlier."

"Oh," Taylor said. "It's fine. The show's about to start anyway, and I should, you know, sit by myself anyway."

"Why?" Selma asked.

"Oh, you know." She lifted her shoulders. "Bait."

"What do you—"

"Come on," Easton said. "We can talk in the back."

"What's going on?" Selma asked as Easton led her toward the dark hall that led to Tyree's office.

"Taylor has a stalker," he said. "And Landon's helping to lure him into the open."

"Oh!"

"That much I can tell you because several people in the bar already know. And I'm also doing some tangential legal work for Taylor. Helping her out of a bind. And that part I can't talk about. Privilege."

"I won't ask." She paused by Tyree's door. "Nice of you to help her out since you have such limited time."

"Selma…"

"It's just—"

"What?" he demanded. "I told you I can't handle the contract."

"Because of us? Or because of your campaign?"

"Does it matter?"

"Probably not," she admitted. "But I still want to know. Call it ego." Or call it libido. Because the more she was around him, the more she realized that legal work was secondary. No, what she wanted was Easton. He'd been on her mind on and off for too long. She'd walked away too fast all those years ago.

Now she wanted to satisfy that craving before she hopped on a plane for Scotland.

A few feet away, Tyree's door snapped open, shooting a wedge of light between them. He looked at her face, then Easton's. "You two heading toward the show?"

"Just clarifying one legal point," Easton said. "Then we'll be there."

"Fair enough," Tyree said, then hurried down the hall toward the bar as Beverly Martin, a rising film star who acted as emcee, started her contest schtick.

"Why are we here?" Easton asked.

And though she hadn't planned this out at all, she took one eager step toward him, rose up on tip toes, and captured his mouth with hers.

At first, he didn't react, and she feared he'd push her away. Then his lips parted and his tongue swept into her mouth, hot and demanding. His arm went around her waist, pulling her close, until their bodies were pressed flat against each other, her breasts hard against his chest—and his cock enticingly hard against her lower belly.

She'd changed clothes for the contest, and she was wearing a black silk tank top with a denim miniskirt that she'd paired with Cuban-style silk stockings and a black garter belt.

His hand thrust beneath her shirt, and his palm against her lower back was making her crazed. Then he started to slide his hand over her ass—and she was certain he'd soon sneak his fingers under her skirt to find her soaking wet and pantyless…

Oh, God, yes, please.

She shifted, spreading her legs just slightly, her own arms going more tightly around his neck as she deepened the kiss, as if she could show him with her tongue what she wanted him to do with his fingers.

But then he broke away, the separation so fast and brutal it was almost painful.

"Jesus, Selma. What are you doing?"

"Me? I think this was definitely a we thing." He didn't answer, and she grimaced. "Fine. I thought you might be more persuaded by action than by words. And besides, you told me you wouldn't take me on as a client. But I don't recall any other protests." She rose up on her toes and kissed him lightly again. "Or am I wrong?"

For a second, she thought that he was going to walk away. But then he took her hand, yanked her close up against his body, but twisted her arm behind her back. He held her that way—trapped, muscles bound and tight—as he bent his head to quickly kiss her.

"We're in public."

"Then you have two choices. Let me go, or take me someplace private." With her free hand, she took his, then guided his hand up her thigh, over the band of the stockings. Then all the way up to her slick, wet core.

He exhaled. The simple sound strained and heavy with eroticism.

"I can't do this. I'm running for office."

"Pretty sure there are lots of politicians who do exactly this." She released his hand and was gratified that his fingers continued to tease her sex. Then she put her fingers to work on his fly, and when it was open she slipped her hand in, intending to set him free.

"*Fuck.*" In one deliberate motion, he stepped back, breaking all contact between them. "Selma, I—I don't know what game you're playing, but no. I'm not getting on the Selma-go-round again. Not when I have so damn much to lose. I really am sorry. I think you know I want you. You've certainly felt the evidence."

And then, for the second time in less than twelve hours, he walked away from her.

As far as Selma was concerned, he'd just thrown down the gauntlet. "Challenge accepted," she whispered. Then walked down the hall as she considered Plan B.

Chapter Five

EASTON'S entire evening could be summed up in one word—frustrating. Not only had Selma given him an inconvenient raging hard-on, but by the time Easton returned to watch the Man of the Month contest, Landon was already being crowned Mr. August—and there'd been no sign of Taylor's stalker.

"Sorry," he'd said to her on the way out. "It seemed like a perfect plan."

She'd shrugged, seeming both disappointed and relieved. And now, in his car, Easton felt essentially the same way, though for entirely different reasons.

He was disappointed that he didn't have Selma naked and beneath him. But he was also relieved to know that he'd made the right decision. Clearly, he had no self-control where Selma Herrington was concerned. She was his Kryptonite, and if he hadn't walked away, God only knew what kind of scandal he'd find himself wrapped up in during this campaign.

So, yeah. Good choice.

Even if it did mean that he was still craving her.

It was a short drive to his house in Rollingwood, a small community in South Austin, and when he pulled into the garage, he was sure of only two things. One, that he needed a long cold shower. And two, that a double bourbon really wasn't going to be enough to take the edge off.

He entered through the utility room, then dumped his briefcase on the bench that lined the hall leading to the butler's pantry before he continued through to the kitchen. Built in the fifties, the original architect had been an admirer of Frank Lloyd Wright, and the house had a contemporary/retro feel. Easton had done very little to it other than update the appliances and put on a fresh coat of paint.

The backyard was a different story. He'd done much of the work himself, working with a few day laborers to build the terraced back yard from the hill that backed up to the rear of the house. Now, he had a wonderful covered patio with an outdoor kitchen, a narrow lap pool with a hot tub on one end, and a stunning garden that rose up to the sky and was filled with flowers and herbs.

He hadn't realized until he'd started house hunting how much the place would mean to him. But after being nomadic with his parents after they lost their business, he'd craved roots. And now, simply walking through the doors of his home made him happy.

And, thanks to the lucrative nature of the career he'd chosen, his parents no longer had to rent. He'd bought them a small home in their Connecticut town, his only regret that they didn't want to move down to Texas where, as they said, they'd never get to watch the seasons change.

In the kitchen, he opened the refrigerator door out of habit, but it wasn't food he wanted, and he continued through the open-style house from kitchen to living room until he reached the built-in bar. He pulled open the cabinet at the bottom and pulled out a bottle of Dusk Flight Rye—ironic, since that was one of Selma's better-selling small-batch labels, and the woman was clinging to his thoughts. But damned if it wasn't his favorite.

The bar had a small ice-maker, and he poured two shots over ice, then pressed the remote to open the blinds that covered the sliding glass doors that made up the entire back wall. He expected to see only the slight dotting of lights that marked the walking path up the terrace. Instead, he saw the unmistakable watery blue glow from the hot tub.

Frowning, he pulled out his phone, wondering if he'd accidentally turned the tub on remotely. But, no, the app was closed.

Someone else had started the tub manually.

And he had a damn good idea who that someone might be.

With a sigh, he slid open the door, then stepped onto the brushed concrete patio. In front of him, the lap pool sat dark, the wind making only the slightest ripples on the water.

To the right, however, blue light filled that corner of the yard, rising from beneath the steaming, bubbling water to cast exotic shadows on the underside of the house's eaves. And there, with water up to her neck and her arms stretched out on either side of her, sat Selma.

Easton pinched the bridge of his nose, then walked toward her. "What the hell are you doing here? For that matter, how did you know where I live?"

Her wet hair was slicked back from her face, and her mascara was running. And when that wide mouth curved into a seductive smile, all Easton could think was that her face was the most erotic thing he'd ever seen. And that, sadly, really wasn't the direction he wanted his thoughts to be going.

"You're in Matthew's contacts," she said. "He shared them with me last year so I could throw him a birthday party. I kept your address." She tilted her head in a casual, flirty way. "I thought I might want it again someday. Guess I was right."

His head was spinning. "And my security? The house and the backyard are all set on an alarm system."

"Yeah, well, I've got mad skills." She flashed a flirty grin. "Don't worry. I didn't go into your house. I was tempted—I'd love to know if your bedroom is the way I imagine it—but I exercised self-restraint."

"That must have been hard," he said dryly.

"Oh, you have no idea."

He spread his hand over his forehead, massaging his temples with his thumb and middle finger. "I think it's time for you to go."

When he looked up, she was staring at him. "Seriously? You didn't used to be so boring. Oh, wait. Yes, you did."

"I think the word you're looking for is responsible."

"Hmmm." Her lips pressed together, and her head tilted as if she was seriously considering his suggestion. "Nope. I'm gonna stick with boring."

"Selma…"

"What?"

"You broke into my yard."

"True. But only because I knew you wouldn't mind."

He resisted the urge to rub his temples again. "Except I do mind."

"Right. Apparently you do." She clicked her tongue

on the roof of her mouth. "So, um, does that mean you want me to leave?"

"Very perceptive of you."

"Oh. Well. Then, fine." She stood up, water sluicing off her naked body as it glistened in that surreal light, making her variety of tattoos stand out. And in that moment, Easton more or less forgot how to breathe.

"Christ, Selma." His voice sounded raw.

"Sorry. I guess responsible means modest, too." She settled back into the water, but it didn't matter. The image of her exceptional body was burned into his mind. Her lush breasts with the dark nipples he wanted to taste. That narrow waist that was the perfect size to slide his hand around. Those long, lean thighs leading up to her bare pussy. His imagination had kicked into overdrive and his body was on fire simply from the fantasies of how she would feel beneath his fingers. How soft her skin would be against his mouth. And how her deep, throaty voice would sound when he made her come so hard she screamed.

She cleared her throat, and when he jumped, she laughed and settled back into the water. "Maybe you ought to bring me a towel. Or you could just join me."

He wished he wasn't so damn tempted, but he forced himself to head toward the cedar-lined chest that held the pool towels. He picked one, then set it on the coping, within easy reach of her.

She sighed. "Come on, Easton. Give me a break. Maybe tonight was a little over the top, but at the end of the day, I'm trying to be responsible, too. I need an attorney. Truly need one. And that's why I came to you."

"There are hundreds of attorneys in this town."

"Yeah, but aren't you the best?"

He said nothing. Just scowled.

She rolled her eyes. "Look, I considered at least half a dozen others, but yours is the name everyone came up with. And yet you won't let me hire you. Not even for a short-term deal that will probably be over even before you officially announce that you're trying for a seat on the bench. Or maybe there's another reason you don't want me to retain you. Maybe you're punishing me for what happened over a decade ago? In which case, that seems petty.

I mean, don't they say we're basically a new person every seven years? And that means you're punishing me for something another person did."

He couldn't help laughing. "I really do love the way you think."

"I just need help. I am who I am, Easton."

"Aimless?"

"More like carefree," she countered.

"Irresponsible?"

"Dammit," she snapped, and he heard real temper in her voice. "I told you. I'm trying to do this right. I want to make sure I get paid well for this deal and they can't screw up the brand I built."

He took a step toward her. "So tell me why you're selling? Because you got lucky and the distillery exploded into a success? Now you're afraid of the hard work it'll take to keep it going? Because that's what you do, isn't it? Walk away before anything gets too real?"

"You know what, Easton? Screw you. I have never been afraid of hard work. *Ever*. Just because I don't want to work in the same damn job in a suit for the rest of my life doesn't mean I'm less than you."

She stood up, her wet, naked body gleaming. "I'll find another damn attorney."

With a violent yank, she wrapped the towel around her and climbed out of the tub. Then she stalked to the small table under the patio covering where she'd left her clothes.

He watched, mesmerized, as she lifted one foot onto the seat of a chair, and, with absolutely no hesitation whatsoever, dried herself from toe to neck.

She took a break long enough to shoot him a glare, then reached for her bra—a retro bullet style–and pulled it on. Next, she fastened a garter belt at her waist, then pulled on her two stockings. He noticed that she didn't pull on any panties, and he didn't see any on his table.

When she started to reach for her skirt, he couldn't take it any more. "Stop."

She looked at him, her expression defiant.

"You're not the least bit self-conscious are you?"

"Why should I be?" she countered. "It's just a body."

He swallowed. "No. It really isn't. Yours is more akin to fine art."

Her lips parted, then closed again, and her tight expression softened. "Thank you."

He took a step toward her, and the closer he got, the more the energy between them crackled. "What if I said I wanted you? Right here. Right now."

She let her gaze roam over him, stopping only briefly at his crotch. "Considering the evidence, I wouldn't be surprised."

"You want me, too."

For a moment, she said nothing. Then she took one step toward him. She took his hand, then slipped their joined fingers between her thighs, moaning as his fingertips found her slick heat. "Yeah," she said. "I guess I do."

He almost lost it right then. Almost pulled her to him, captured her in a kiss, and then bent her over the table and buried himself in her.

It was a testament to his willpower that he didn't.

Instead, he stood frozen, watching her lips and that fuckable mouth of hers.

She said nothing, but slowly lifted that same hand to her mouth and sucked so hard on his wet finger that it almost felt as if her mouth were on his cock. When she pulled away, her smile held a hint of victory. "But someone once told me that there's a difference between want and willpower."

"Whoever that was, he was a fucking idiot," Easton said, and she burst out laughing.

"I have an idea." She stepped closer, her palm cupping him. "You're a pragmatic guy. This is a fast deal I need negotiated. And we're obviously stuck in each other's heads. So we bend our rules. You take my case. And I won't scurry away. We fuck like bunnies. Get each other completely out of our systems. And this deal comes with a no-risk guarantee, because we know that in the end, I'm selling my business and moving to Scotland."

She slowly stroked his cock, rock hard now under the suit trousers he still wore. Slowly, she sank to her knees, her fingers tugging at his fly. "What do you say? As far as torrid affairs go, it couldn't be cleaner."

A voice in his head yelled that he was going to regret this. But all Easton did was twine his fingers in her hair and tilt his head back to the stars as she took him in her mouth. "Yeah," he gasped, grasping the side of the table for balance. "I think we have a deal."

Chapter Six

SELMA FREED HIS COCK, hard and ridged and absolutely perfect. She held him in her hand, enjoying the power of knowing that she had the ability to bring this man to his knees. She licked him first, reveling in the way his body tightened, the fact that she was bringing him pleasure exciting her. And when he twined his hands in her hair and guided her mouth to his cock, she enjoyed it all the more.

She wanted it wild. Wanted to be his. To surrender to his whims. To please him and have him use her, knowing that her turn would come next and he would take her all the way to the stars.

Even after so many years, she remembered the feel

of him. The taste of him. He'd been a skilled lover when he was in law school. A touch could make her wet. A brush of his tongue could make her come. But he hadn't developed the edge yet, and the Easton who stood before her now was a man with all sorts of edges. The kind who could take a girl to dark places, then fill them with light.

God, how she wanted that.

He thrust into her faster, and she clung to his butt, holding him in place, wishing he'd shed the pants. She wanted the feel of skin on skin. She wanted all of him.

"Baby, that feels so good. I'm so damn close."

She sucked harder, but he gently pulled out. "I want to feel you. I want to feel *us*."

And then, as if to prove that he was echoing her thoughts, he added, "I want out of these damn clothes." Quickly, he stripped off his pants and jacket, but kept the suit shirt on. She almost insisted he take it off, then thought better of it. She liked the way he looked with his rock hard cock peeking out from the shirt tails. Just looking at him made her aroused, and she was already so close.

"Please," she said, then started to reach back to unfasten her garter.

"Oh, no. That is too perfect. Bend over."

"What?"

He smacked her rear lightly, and she almost passed out from lust. "I said to bend over."

She did, holding onto the edges of the small round table, her breasts against the cool tile and her ass presented for him.

"You're so gorgeous. Spread your legs."

She did as he said, and he slid his cock up and down her crack, teasing her pussy until it took all of her willpower not to reach back and touch herself.

Then again …

She slid one hand between her legs and started to stroke her clit as he teased her with the tip of his cock.

"That's so hot," he said. "Don't stop doing that."

"No, sir," she said, then smiled when he moaned. Apparently he liked the game as much as she did. "Fuck me, please." She was so turned on her muscles were clenching, desperate to pull him in. "I need you inside me."

"Anything you want. Hang on."

She didn't want to hang on at all. She wanted everything, and she wanted it now. But she told herself that good things came to those who wait and so she patiently waited as he pulled a condom from his wallet then sheathed himself. His hand slicked over her, and he moaned. "You're so wet," he said. "I'm going to fuck you so deep."

"Yes." It was all she could manage. Words seemed beyond her. She'd moved on to sensations only.

And then she felt the sensation of him. The pressure at her entrance, and then the intensity of his first thrust inside her. She closed her eyes, reveling in the feel of him. The way he filled her. Claimed her. And when he started to rhythmically thrust inside her, all rational thought left her and she knew only the exceptional growing sensation of a powerful orgasm rising inside her, borne of the wild, deep thrusts of his cock and the firm teasing of her clit with her own fingers.

More and more, deeper and deeper. She felt his body tighten inside her. Felt his muscles tense around her. He reached out and grabbed her neck, lifting her head so that he was holding her tight, her breasts off the table now. He was riding her, her body entirely at his mercy.

"Come for me."

"Please," she said. "More."

He teased her ass with his free hand. "Is this more?" he whispered. "Or how about this?" he asked, then licked the curve of her ear. "Come now," he ordered. "I want to feel you explode."

His breath teased her ear as he spoke, and that was the final push. Fingers of electricity shot through her body, each strand racing toward her core. She felt alive, on fire. She felt like pure energy, the stars, the big fucking bang.

"Now," he urged. "Go over now."

As if she had no choice but to obey this man, she felt the world fall out from under her. She exploded. She broke apart. She touched the heavens.

And then ever so gently, she fell back to the earth and into his arms.

HE RELISHED her warmth as they curled up together in bed. He'd carried her there, and now he wanted nothing more than to hold her close and keep her safe. His fingers danced lazily against her skin, pausing at the tattoo beneath her breast, just over her heart. *Please*.

"What does it mean?"

She snuggled close. "I'll tell you later. Right now, I want to know how you're going to negotiate my deal."

He laughed, but was happy to oblige, and so he asked her to outline the deal so far. She did, and he listened, asking questions and ending up pleasantly surprised by the thoughtfulness of her answers and the fact that she'd obviously done her homework.

"Well, my first priority is to get you as much cash as possible. Once it's done, you're pretty much out of the picture. They're buying your brand, which means you're done. If they fuck it up, your only recourse is the satisfaction of a full bank account."

She frowned. "I don't like the sound of that."

"Not much way around it, but I'll do some thinking.

I want you as protected as possible. And it's all about negotiation. You never know until you try."

"You sound like you enjoy it."

"I do."

"Is that the kind of thing you can do as a judge?"

He considered the question, surprised by the lump that formed in his stomach. "Honestly, not really. As a mediator, yeah. But a judge has a different rulebook."

"Then why do you want to do it?"

Another hard question. Apparently the girl didn't throw soft balls. "There's prestige, of course."

"That doesn't seem like your bag."

"No, but it gives you some power. To make change, I mean."

"I thought judges only interpreted the law," she countered. "Wouldn't being in the legislature make more sense if you wanted to bring about change?"

He couldn't deny she had a point.

"Then why are you running for judge and not just

staying in your practice? Or maybe trying to be a senator?"

Since that wasn't a question he felt like he could answer when he was overtired and oversexed, he turned the tables. "Why are you selling the distillery?"

Her laugh was like the ringing of bells. "Oh, that's because I want to." She grinned. "I want to do this, too."

With a quick movement, she straddled him, then grinned before she slowly eased down his body to once again take his cock into her mouth. He wanted to call her out for avoiding the question, but he wanted more to savor the feel of her hot little mouth doing wonderful things to his body.

She pulled away far too soon for his taste, but when she replaced her mouth with her pussy, riding him hard and fast and taking him to the edge, he really couldn't complain. Especially when she made him come so hard he thought he might bruise his throat when he cried out in pleasure.

And then, when she whispered, "Ready for another round?" his eager cock twitched and perked up all over again.

She would, he thought, be the death of him.

By four o'clock in the morning, they'd finally worn each other out, and he gently kissed her temple as she fell asleep in his arms.

By five, he had to get up to catch a plane.

He'd never once left a woman in his bed when he wasn't home. And yet he didn't even blink at the thought of leaving Selma.

And instead of kicking her out, he simply brushed a kiss over her cheek and whispered to her sleeping form that she could stay as long as she wanted.

Chapter Seven

"YOU JUST SPENT an hour working out, and now you're eating that?" Selma wrinkled her nose at the pile of pancakes, side of bacon, omelet, and hash browns that the waitress slid in front of Matthew. They were at Magnolia Cafe on South Congress, her brother was completely pigging out, and she was indulging in one measly breakfast taco.

Okay, not *that* measly since the portions at Magnolia were huge. But Matthew's breakfast could feed a small family.

"That's why I need a big breakfast," Matthew said. "And you know I don't eat like this all the time."

True enough. Usually he ate a training diet she found both strange and unappealing. But when they did their semi-regular breakfasts together, he went all out. As evidenced by the mass quantities of carbs sitting in front of him at the moment.

"Besides," he added, "if *you* would work out, you wouldn't feel like you have to live on salads."

"Hello? Do you see the giant breakfast taco? And I don't live on salads. But they're my staple so that when I get a whim for something decadent, I have no guilt."

He stabbed a huge chunk of pancakes with his fork. "Fair enough. But exercise erases guilt, too. And, hey, you have a brother who owns a gym. I can hook you up with all the good machines."

She rolled her eyes. "I get plenty of exercise. In fact, I got an excellent workout last night."

A *very* excellent workout, and for a moment, she allowed herself to savor the memory. Even this morning had been incredible. He'd let her stay the night—which, considering how they'd started out, seemed almost miraculous—but he'd had to leave early to catch a plane to Dallas. And instead of kicking her out, he'd simply brushed a kiss over her cheek and told her to stay as long as she wanted.

If it hadn't been for her brother, she might still be naked in the sheets, waiting for him to come back.

The thought made her sigh, and when she did, Matthew narrowed his eyes and put his fork down.

"Easton? Oh, man, Selma. What the hell are you doing getting involved with him? You told me this morning that he'd agreed to sign on as your attorney. You didn't say you were sleeping with him."

"If it matters, we didn't sleep much."

"Don't even joke. Come on, Selma. You know that's just bad business."

"Trust me. It's fine. *I'm* fine." She reached over the table and snagged one of his pieces of bacon. "But thanks for caring."

He rolled his eyes, but the truth was they both probably cared too much. After all, at the end of the day, it was Matthew and Selma against the world. Because while they both loved their parents dearly, Selma and her brother had literally survived hell together. Beatings, weeks of nothing but water and saltines. And day after day after day of being told they were worthless. That they were only in the way.

It had gotten a little better when their birth father had disappeared. At least the maternal unit didn't bloody their backs with a leather belt. Mostly, she just ignored them. But when she'd run out of money, she'd gone to local shelters for help, and that had been when things started to look up. There'd been other adults who'd warmed to them, and Matthew and Selma let those grown-ups get close to their hearts.

But then their bio-mom would rip them out of that shelter and move them across town or across the state. Everywhere they went, they left a trail of people who might have cared for them, if they'd been able to stay long enough. Instead, they ended up in Austin, alone. Just Matthew and Selma and their birth mom.

Then even she'd walked away, and after that moment it really was Matthew and Selma against the world.

Even when the Herringtons had plucked them out of foster care, it had been hard to get close. At least for Selma. Somehow, she'd always been waiting for the other shoe to drop.

Honestly, maybe she still was.

Selma sighed, then took a contemplative sip of coffee. Yeah, she was screwed up. But by all rights, she should be a hell of a lot worse.

She stabbed a clump of sausage out of her taco with her fork, then looked up to find Matthew staring at her. "What?"

"It's not fine, Selma."

"Come on, Matthew. For once, just trust me. I'm thirty-five. I promise you I can take care of myself."

He started to respond, but she shook her head firmly.

"No. Moving on. Total change of topic. Have you talked to Mom and Dad? They called me the day before yesterday, but I couldn't hear a thing. Where are they now?"

"China. Can you believe it? Mom emailed me last night. They're traveling from Beijing up to Shanghai."

Their parents—the only people in her life who deserved to be called parents—had recently set out on a five-month adventure to see the world. "See," Selma said. "They're spontaneous. It's not just me."

"Sure they are. If you consider four years of planning spontaneous."

"A fair point. But what about you? Aren't you being uncharacteristically spontaneous?"

"You mean about the gym?"

She nodded. They'd met this morning at his downtown gym on Lavaca like they always did before grabbing breakfast together. But instead of leaving right away, as was their habit, he'd taken her into the bowels of the gym. He'd talked to her about the various machines and their cost. About the floorplan of the building. About his membership stats.

And then he told her that he was going to move forward with franchising.

He already had several locations around Austin, and he oversaw all of them, using managers for the day-to-day stuff. And, sure, he'd talked about franchising, but she'd assumed that was a lark.

But today, he was talking as if it was really happening. With lawyers and paperwork and money flowing.

"Are you sure you want to do that?" she asked. "I

mean, not to rain on your parade, but are you sure?"

"Yeah," he said, without the slightest hesitation. "Why wouldn't I be?"

"I don't know. It's such a permanent step. What if it falls apart?"

"Why should it?"

"I don't know. Because something happens."

He nodded slowly. "You do understand that at the end of the day, I'm the glue that holds the whole chain together. There's no one I trust more than myself. Not even you."

"Yay for self-confidence, but you know that things won't always turn out the way you want them to. You'll get it going and then, boom, it'll get pulled out from under you. Nothing is ever solid."

"Maybe not. But it's worth trying to be." He tilted his head as he eyed her. "Are you nervous for me?"

"Always," she admitted.

"Do you think I can do it?"

"You're one of those guys who can do anything."

"Except, apparently, find a good woman."

"You will," she said firmly. "One who deserves you." Her phone chirped, and she frowned at her brother. "That's my alarm. I have to run. Free-Tail is one of the sponsors for tonight's event at the Winston Hotel, and I've got temporary waiters coming in I have to train."

"Go for it. I'll sit here in peace and finish my mountain of pancakes."

She slid out of the booth.

"Hey." His single word stopped her.

"What?"

"You can do anything, too," Matthew said.

"I know. And that means I can also do everything." She winked, then turned and hurried for the door.

THE LAST THING Easton had wanted after his unexpected night of debauchery and sin was to leave a warm and willing woman in his bed so that he could fly up to Dallas for hours of mind-numbing depositions. Especially since, when he'd finally returned home at just after five in the evening, the sheets had turned cold and she was nowhere to be found.

The second to last thing he wanted to do after a night of wild, acrobatic sex chased by mundane depositions, was to be standing in the grand ball-room of the Winston Hotel in Austin, trying to kick-start enough brain cells to allow him to make conversation. And yet here he was, standing right inside the doorway leading to one of the many charity balls that served to get his name in front of voters and influencers with as much efficiency as a finger swipe on Tinder.

And considering he could barely walk straight today, he wanted to be here even less.

Still, Easton had a goal, and he and Judge Coale had a plan for reaching that goal. Which meant that despite the fact that Selma had essentially ridden him to the moon and wrung him dry, he was at this party to work.

He drew a breath, straightened his tie, and stepped the rest of the way into the chaos of the ballroom. Immediately, a waitress in a black tank top handed him a glass of bourbon, and he took a sip, impressed by the smooth taste with just enough burn to make it worth drinking. He looked up, realized the waitress's tank top had the Free-Tail logo on it, and froze. Because there she was. *Selma*. On the other side of the ballroom.

In a sea of business suits and conservative dresses, Selma Herrington stood out like a sexy sore thumb. She wore skintight leather black pants paired with the same logo tank top as her staff. A red belt accentuated her small waist, and her legs seemed all the longer in her four-inch heels. She wore a retro style bullet bra underneath the top, a look that some modern men probably didn't care for, but that he thought was erotic as hell, a fact proven out by the tightening in his balls, both from the sight of her now and the memory of how she looked last night in nothing but that bra, stockings, and a garter belt.

Her lips were painted fire-engine red and her short hair was spiky now and tipped with pink and green instead of the previous blue.

She looked sexy as hell, wild as a forest fire, and completely out of place.

She was also heading straight for him. A fact that his body fully appreciated. But that made his inner politician cringe.

"Hello, lover," she purred as she approached.

"Christ, Selma, keep your voice down."

"I enjoyed last night."

He swallowed. "So did I."

Her smile was smug. "I know."

"Why are you here?"

Her brows rose, but he wasn't sure if she was offended or amused. "That's my whiskey you're drinking. We're one of the sponsors of the benefit."

"Of course. I wasn't thinking." He drew in a breath, forcing himself not to reach out even as he told himself that starting this arrangement with her was a bad idea. Because clearly he was incapable of being around her without wanting to touch her. "Listen, Selma, I need to mingle. I'm going to be announcing soon, and I should do the meet-and-greet before the speeches start."

"Meet me in the ladies' lounge in fifteen."

He blinked at her. "What?"

She leaned closer and, thankfully, lowered her voice. "I have this feeling that you've never fucked in the ladies room during a party. I assumed it was on your bucket list."

"Selma…"

"I want your cock in my mouth again," she said, and he almost groaned aloud. "Or anywhere else you want to put it."

Oh, dear Lord, he was done for.

"Selma, stop. We had an arrangement. And you know I can't."

She lifted a shoulder. "You'd be amazed how much you can do if you just step outside your box. Your box is pretty tight, Easton. I'm just trying to help you push back those walls." She stepped away, then blew him a kiss. "I'll be there in fifteen. Hopefully you will be, too."

"Don't bet the ranch," he said. But as he looked around the mind numbingly dull party … as his mind started to imagine the sight of Selma on her knees as he fucked her mouth …

Oh, God.

He wouldn't go.

He couldn't.

But a small part of him damn sure wanted to.

Chapter Eight

DAMN HIM.

For three full minutes—he'd counted them—Easton had been talking himself in and out of going to that bathroom. What was wrong with him? He didn't usually act so impulsively, and he could only assume that Selma had put a spell on him. She certainly had the power to make him lose his mind.

He thought of last night with her and smiled. *Yeah, she definitely held some power.*

"Thinking about winning the election?"

Immediately, the smile left his lips, and he shifted to face Marianne more directly. "I didn't see you there," he said.

"Daydreaming, I suppose." Her smile was both sweet and flirty, and he felt a moment of guilt for having no interest in her whatsoever. Not sexually and not as a colleague. Judge Coale might think she was a good wingman, but he found her to be more like mashed potatoes—no personality of her own.

Selma, though …

"Marianne, I'm so sorry. There's someone I need to go talk to."

He should mingle. He should play the game. He should schmooze and do all those things.

All he wanted to do was find the girl.

All he cared about was letting his goddamn cock rule the show.

At the moment, he was okay with that.

He slipped away to the hall with the restrooms, then looked back before easing into the ladies lounge. It had multiple stalls, but Selma was leaning against the row of sinks smiling at him.

"We're alone," she said. "Lock the door."

He lifted a brow, certain they were going to get

caught. And then—because he was clearly under a spell—he did as she said.

She crooked a finger, and he walked to her, but when she started to drop to her knees, he shook his head. "No. My turn."

"Really?" Her brows went up.

He grinned. "You've corrupted me. Might as well go all the way."

He looked around, then nodded to the sink. "Sit up there on the counter. Then pull down those leather pants."

She bit her lower lip, then leaned forward. "Why, Your Honor? Are you in the mood to eat pussy?"

His balls tightened, and he pulled her close, then kissed that dirty little mouth.

"On the counter," he ordered. "Now."

"I hear applause," she said. "That means people will be coming. Folks always slip away when the speeches start."

"Then we need to hurry," he said, relishing the feeling of being wild. Of going a little crazy.

"You're a bad influence," he said as she shimmied her pants down, then planted her bare ass on the counter. She spread her knees, and he licked his lips.

"I want your tongue," she said, slipping a finger inside her.

He heard high heels in the hallway.

"Fuck," she said, but he leaned forward and kissed her, then bent lower, roughly pulling her sex toward his mouth. Then he closed his mouth over the sweet, sensual taste of her. His tongue filling her, his teeth nipping at her clit.

She squirmed, her hands tightening in his hair, her sex bucking against his face. "Fuck, yes," she moaned, her voice a stage whisper. "Oh, God, I'm close."

He reached around, sucking her more and more as he slid a finger around and found her ass. He penetrated her and she swallowed a scream, then screamed again as he hit the sweet spot and she exploded, a flood of her sweet juices rushing over his tongue.

He stood, then kissed her. "You taste fucking delicious. And you're either going to be the best thing that ever happened to me or the end of my career."

She winked. "Maybe I'll be both and we can run off to Bora Bora."

He laughed, but at the moment long hot days of lazy sex seemed like a fabulous idea.

A pounding at the door made them both jump, and she slid off the counter, their eyes locking and full of laughter. She held her finger to her lips, then fixed her clothes.

"Could someone please unlock this door?"

"Coming," she trilled, then hurried that way, with his hand tight in hers.

"What are you doing?" he whispered, but she didn't answer. Just unlocked the door and tugged it open.

"Was it stuck?" she asked innocently, her eyes on the petite elderly woman clutching her purse.

"It was locked."

"No ma'am. I just pulled really hard." She smiled brilliantly. "Glad I was here to help. Oh, and sir," she added, turning to him with an even bigger smile. "Thank you so, so much."

She met the lady's eyes again as Easton's head spun. "This nice gentleman helped me get my ring back." She pointed to a small pinkie ring he hadn't noticed. "I'd dropped it down the sink. It was my grandmother's. I couldn't bear to lose it."

"What a nice young man," the lady said to Easton, who could only nod silently and think that ever since he'd met Selma again, he'd been living in a world gone mad.

Chapter Nine

ON FRIDAY, Selma arrived at Easton's office by eight and they were settled into a conference room by eight-fifteen, fortified with a huge pot of coffee, a tray of bagels with various spreads, and two huge bowls of fresh fruit.

By ten, their private buffet looked like a troop of hungry Boy Scouts had been at it, and the formerly pristine conference table was littered with printouts, marked up pages, yellow legal pads, and coffee cups. She'd kicked off her shoes and had tossed her button-down aside, so that she was wearing only jeans and a tank top. Easton, however, still looked perfectly put together in his gray suit.

"I still think the up-front payment should be higher," he said, tapping his pen as he frowned at the contract. "But if they're going to lowball you, then the royalty needs to go way up."

"Either way, it's a lot of money." She climbed onto the credenza and swung her bare feet, then smiled at one of the attorneys walking by, who was peering in the window at her.

"Yes, but it's your money. You've earned it by putting value into your business. If they want to buy the business, they need to pay you for that value."

"I get it. I do. But it's still more money than I ever thought I'd be able to sell my tiny little distillery for."

"Your tiny little place has developed a big reputation. And that's because of your hard work. Don't sell yourself short."

She was about to tell him that she wouldn't when the door opened and a woman stepped in looking as if she'd just walked off a magazine ad for *Corporate Woman*, assuming there even was such a magazine.

"Sorry for interrupting. I have to leave early and

just wanted to make sure we're driving together to the ranch tomorrow."

Selma sat up straighter, feeling suddenly inadequate and left out. Which was ridiculous. She had no claim on Easton. And, honestly, she didn't want one. Why would she when she was leaving for Scotland soon?

"Honestly, I hadn't thought about it," Easton said, barely looking up from the papers. He lifted his head, considering her the same way that she'd noticed he considered the validity of a point on the contract. "Sure. Of course. I'll pick you up around one, okay?"

Her smile blossomed. "Perfect." She glanced toward Selma. "I'm sorry. We didn't meet. I'm Marianne, one of the senior associates in the firm."

"Selma. One of the clients in the firm."

Marianne's laugh sounded genuinely amused. "You're in good hands with Easton. Sorry again for interrupting."

"Not a problem," Selma said, unnerved by the relief that had washed over her from knowing that she was a co-worker and not a personal, intimate friend.

Ridiculous. What did she have to be jealous of?

But then the receptionist buzzed to tell him that a woman named Hannah Donovan had stopped by to see if he wanted to join her for lunch, and Selma knew that, rational or not, she was jealous.

Absurd.

Of course it wasn't really about him. Not directly. On the contrary, she was jealously protecting their plan to fuck each other out of their systems as he worked on her deal to sell the distillery. It really wasn't personal.

"Selma?"

She snapped to attention. "What?"

"I was just saying sorry for the interruptions, but it looks like you need it. Are you getting tired?"

"My mind's getting a little fried from all the legalese you're tossing at me. But it's okay."

"Why don't we continue at your place?"

Her brows rose. "My apartment?"

"Your distillery."

"Oh!" She loved that idea. She was ridiculously proud of the distillery and the idea of showing it off to him pleased her more than it probably should. "Let's go."

THE DISTILLERY WAS LOCATED in a small building in East Austin that she'd bought with money she'd borrowed from Matthew. But Free-Tail was doing so well, that she'd been able to pay him back every dime.

"It's not much to look at," she told him as they entered. "The front room is for retail, though I don't do a lot of walk-in business." She led him into the back, introducing him to her small staff as they went, then showing him her equipment and her aging vats.

"It takes a while to age whiskey traditionally," she told him. "But I've been distilling since I was about eighteen, and I've learned a few tricks. And I started by selling some distilled spirits that don't need to be aged, then graduated up to my whiskeys."

"But in five years?"

"I experimented." Her voice was casual, but she was proud of what she'd accomplished. "I talked with some engineers and worked on a system that allows for quick aging." She nodded toward the big silver box on one side of the cavernous room. "It's all about pressure. And I use special vats with oak cut up inside in that monster over there. Then after that, we move the product to finishing barrels."

"That's amazing."

She shrugged. "That's the thing with craft distilleries these days—using local ingredients and shortening the aging time. I'm not the only one, but I did come up with my system."

"Which also explains why Penoldi-Gryce wants to buy you out," he added, referring to the company with which they were negotiating. "They want your tech."

She nodded as she looked around the room. "It'll be weird not coming here every day. But at least I know that the whiskey I've crafted will continue."

He stepped behind her and put his hand on her

shoulder. "You don't actually know that," he said gently.

She frowned, twisting around to see him.

"Once they buy, they have control. They'll keep your brand, but ultimately, they can make what they want. And they may even ditch your label after a while.

"Oh." She bit her lip. "Well, I guess that makes sense."

She shrugged out from his hand and went to sit on a small bench by her primary processing machine. "And if they don't ditch it, they get to use my label on their new stuff."

It wasn't a question, but when he sat next to her, he offered an answer anyway. "They will."

She sat, digesting that. She'd known it, of course. But somehow the truth was sinking in deeper.

For a moment, they sat quietly. Then Easton spoke, his voice so low she almost had to strain to hear him. "My parents had a place. Not a distillery, of course, but a hamburger stand. I watched them lose it. Just ripped out from under them. And when they did, I swear they lost a piece of themselves. It's part of why I became a lawyer."

She licked her lips. "Why are you telling me this?"

"No reason. Just the way you talk about this place reminds me of the way they talked."

"Thanks, but it's different. I'm making a choice. They got it taken away." She turned to meet his sympathetic eyes. "You get the difference, right? Choice is what matters."

"Can't argue there. You sound like you know what you're talking about."

"I have some experience with having the world ripped out from under me," she admitted, then regretted the words. He'd ask what she meant, of course.

But he didn't. Instead, he studied her face. Then he simply nodded, and for a moment she felt a wave of disappointment followed by the shocking realization that she'd not only expected the question, but she'd wanted it. Wanted to share her past—her screwed up history—with him.

Unnerved, she stood up.

"Selma?" When she didn't turn, he continued. "We need to think about your counter offer. If you coming on board isn't part of the deal—and you've told me you just want to walk away—then we can only limit their ability to use the brand in a very minute fashion. At least, if we want the deal to happen."

"Then I want money," she said, her stomach tight. "If they get the ability to do whatever they want, then I want loads of cash."

"Yeah," he said, rising and putting a hand on her shoulder. "Sounds like we're both on the same page."

Chapter Ten

UNITED STATES SENATOR DOUGLAS TODD had represented the great state of Texas for going on fifteen years, and according to Judge Coale, his support would be invaluable as Easton moved up the ladder, hopefully to a federally appointed seat on an appellate or district court.

That goal was years away, but navigating the judicial waters required long-term planning.

Which was why Easton was sitting in Jeffries, one of Austin's finest restaurants, sharing dinner with the man even though he'd much rather be at home in the hot tub with Selma celebrating the excellent counteroffer they'd put together and faxed over to Penoldi-Gryce's attorneys that afternoon.

Not that he should complain. These kinds of dinners came with the territory. And Senator Todd really had led a fascinating life. Unfortunately, he didn't have a clue how to tell it, and he made his time in the military and the CIA sound like an advertisement for motor oil.

It was all Easton could do not to fall asleep. And, frankly, he was working harder to look interested than he'd ever remembered working in his life. More to the point, the senator seemed entirely uninterested in getting to know him, which seemed counter to the reason that they were having dinner. Because how could Todd get behind Easton as an up-and-coming player in the judiciary if Todd didn't know a thing about him?

Easton didn't know. Frankly, he didn't care, though he would definitely bend Judge Coale's ear later.

Right then, all he wanted was to get home. And if he got out of there early enough, he might even go see Selma. After all, they had a deal, and today had been solely about the work. Time to add some balance to the equation.

"And about that time, I realized that the initiative

wouldn't go through if I didn't put all my weight behind it," the senator said.

Easton had entirely lost the thread of the conversation, but was saved when his phone chimed.

"I'm so sorry," he said, pulling it out. "I usually silence this, but my mother is ill." A huge lie, and he owed his mom a phone call to make up for using her as his foil. But right then, he didn't care who was texting. He opened the app, checked the screen, and almost lost it right there.

Selma. Entirely naked and twisted up in her sheets just enough to be completely immodest and yet not look like porn. In fact, to Easton, she looked like dessert.

Below the picture, her text read - *Wanna play?*

Oh, yes. Did he ever.

Who took that picture?

That wasn't what he'd intended to ask, but jealousy had prompted his fingers.

That's what tripods and remote shutter clickers are for. I want you. And I wanted you to know.

Relief that it wasn't an old picture some other man

had taken—or worse, that there was someone else with her—crashed over him with unexpected force.

My house. One hour. I want you like that.

Holy hell, what was he doing? *Sexting* in one of the city's nicest and most established restaurants? While he was schmoozing a United States Senator? This was not the Easton he'd become over the last two years as his plan to go after a judicial seat had evolved. And this definitely was not the path that was going to get him elected.

But it could only screw him up if someone found out. And he'd been walking the straight-and-narrow for so long now, that he could handle a respite. A small break into the wild and dark. After all, Selma wasn't a permanent fixture. She was a pressure valve. A temporary necessity.

And, frankly, considering tonight, she was a welcome escape hatch.

"Senator, I'm so sorry, but I won't be able to stay for dessert and coffee. I need to get home and take care of some family matters."

EASTON WOKE WITH THE SUN, then rolled over, breathless and sated, as Selma curled up next to him. She'd met him at the door as he'd walked in, racing naked across his living room and launching herself into his arms.

He'd taken her on the floor, fast and hard, before they'd moved to the bed for a repeat performance, that time focusing on slow and easy. She was, by far, the most responsive, aggressive, sexy, fascinating woman he'd ever met, and he had absolutely no regrets about ditching the senator.

He was, however, starting to wonder about where they would go from here. Because when he thought about not having her in his life…

Well, honestly, he *didn't* think about it. Because he simply didn't like the concept of that reality.

Her fingers trailed over his chest, tracing patterns down to his abs. "You're thinking too loud," she said. "Wanna share?"

"I was wondering if you want to come to the benefit tonight," he said, the idea springing into his mind. "It's for literacy, and it's at the landfill."

She sat up, completely oblivious to the way the sheet fell off of her. "Excuse me?"

"Texas Disposal Systems maintains an exotic ranch right next to the landfill. It's their way of giving back. It's not open to the public, but they rent the Pavillion out for events."

"That's completely cool. And I could see the animals?"

"Absolutely."

"But are you sure I can go? I mean, as your date?"

Regret stabbed through him. "Probably not. But I have an extra ticket. And you can be one of the guests. Someone I have to schmooze for later votes."

She laughed, then moved to straddle him. "I don't know. You schmoozed me pretty good already. I have no more votes to give."

He cupped her ass. "Right now, neither do I. But later I hope for a lot more schmoozing."

"Deal." She slid off him, then rolled off the bed. "I need to take a shower and get out of here. When is this thing?"

He sat up, more disturbed than he should be that she was leaving. Hell, he'd practically ordered her here last night without even thinking to ask if she had other plans. "Seven," he said. "You can't stay for breakfast?"

"I was going to grab a coffee and a donut on the way." She tilted her head. "Do you want to join me?"

"It's not even nine on a Saturday. Where are you going?" he asked, but she just smiled.

"Why don't we start in the shower, and you'll learn the rest when we get there?"

THERE TURNED out to be San Gabriel Park in Georgetown, a town about thirty minutes outside of Austin, where dozens of children under the age of thirteen were running from bouncy houses to craft stations to makeshift photo booths.

"What is this?" Easton asked as they walked from the car to the mass of kids.

"I work with an organization that takes foster kids out on excursions. Some foster parents can't afford to do much of that or are just overwhelmed. This gives the kids some interaction and the parents can come, too, if it works for them."

He glanced sideways at her. "That sounds like a great cause."

She shrugged. "There's a need."

They'd reached a small cluster of adults, so he didn't ask her about the tightness in her tone of voice. Instead, he accepted an assignment to go play catch with a group of young boys while Selma set up at a face-painting station and started to decorate a very long line of little girls.

By the end of an hour, Easton was exhausted, and begged the boys to stop for a bit. Instead of catch, he took them down to the river's edge. A few of the kids and chaperones were already there with stale bread for the ducks, many of which were so tame they ate right out of the kids' hands.

"You're really a lawyer?" A tall boy of eleven who'd told Easton he was Alfonse stood with his hands on his hips as he focused on Easton's face.

"I am."

"That's what I'm going to do, too. My dad beat up

my mom. He's in jail and she can't take care of me anymore. I'm gonna be a prosecutor."

Easton's gut twisted with the kid's words, but he tried not to show it. But dear God, he'd thought his childhood with his parents' legal and financial problems had been rough? Talk about foolish. "I think you'll make a great prosecutor. You know what justice is and you've seen what prosecutors are fighting for."

The kid grinned, as if Easton had just anointed him as a district attorney right then.

"Yeah. My dad's a prick. But Gary's okay."

"Gary?"

"My foster father. He and Jessie are gonna try to adopt me." His smile was wide, but a little sad. "They want me. My dad didn't. And my mom?" He shrugged. "I don't think she really did, either. But at least she never hit me."

Dear God. What the hell could he say to this kid?

"Alfonse, everybody has a path. Some start out pretty crooked. But it sounds like yours is straightening out. Here," he added, then fished out his wallet and handed the kid his business card. "You keep in touch. I mean it."

The boy's face lit up, and he tucked the card in his back pocket before rushing to the riverbank to join a group of kids who were calling his name.

Easton went to the check-in desk and downed three glasses of water, his mind spinning.

He spent the next two hours on auto-pilot, but when they were back in the car, he'd processed enough to turn to Selma when they reached a red light. "Those kids—they have it pretty rough."

"Yup."

"Was that you?" he asked gently.

She didn't answer, and the light turned green. He continued on in silence, angry with himself for getting personal. Obviously, that wasn't where she wanted to go with him.

He pulled into his garage, then killed the engine. "Do you want to come in? Or are you heading home? You're still coming to the benefit tonight, right?"

She turned to look at him, her brow furrowed. Then she pulled off the plain white t-shirt she wore. There was nothing sexual about the act, and he wasn't surprised when she pointed to the small tattoo beneath her left breast, near her heart. The single word, *please*.

"You asked me about it, remember?"

He nodded.

"It was my first tattoo. I was twelve. Matthew and I had been in foster care for a while, and then we learned that the Herringtons wanted to adopt us. I snuck out of the house that very first night and managed to get to a tattoo parlor. I looked older than my age, and they didn't ask for ID—it's probably a miracle I didn't get hepatitis from the needle, the place was skanky. Anyway, that's what I got. That word over my heart. Please. *Please* let them be the ones. *Please* let it last."

Let it last. The words echoed like a clue in his mind.

"Did they ever find out you snuck out?"

She nodded. "Oh, yeah. My second day in their house and I got grounded. I figured that was the end. But then things moved on. I was so sure the end was coming—it always did—and then we were in front of a judge and they were officially my parents. My head totally spun."

"And now?"

Her laugh was harsh. "Now I know that I have a good thing—but I still expect it to come crashing down. I'm a glass half empty girl. Matthew is convinced we paid our dues and found Shangri-La. He's a glass half full guy."

He exhaled, lost under the weight of her story and Alfonse's dark, hopeful eyes. "I'm sorry you're still not sure." He took her hand. "Maybe one day you'll stop believing that the ground is going to fall out from under you."

"Maybe," she agreed. "But I'm not holding my breath."

Chapter Eleven

SELMA HADN'T EXPECTED the landfill to be as cool as it was. Somehow, her head hadn't managed to put together *exotic animals* and *trash*. But once she was there, she was mesmerized by the zebras, rhinoceroses, tigers, and other wildlife that she saw on the brief guided tour that the benefit guests were offered.

Since she wasn't technically there with Easton, she'd been in a different tour group, and now she was back in the pavilion, wandering the various tables— some offering information about literacy, some displaying the items donated for the silent auction— and sipping her glass of Chardonnay.

Honestly, while she thought literacy was a great

cause, after her time with the animals, she was bored. A state of affairs she was certain would be remedied if Easton were beside her.

He, however, was nowhere to be found. Or at least, she corrected, he *hadn't been*. Now, she caught a glimpse of his dark hair and broad shoulders through the window, and she forced herself to walk toward the main door instead of skipping like an eager puppy.

She stopped short, however, when he stepped inside. Marianne was on his arm, her face lit up with pleasure.

Angry green monsters started to claw at Selma's insides, and she told herself sternly that she was being stupid. She had no right to be jealous. They were coworkers. She'd known they were coming to this together. He was running for judge. Of course he needed someone like Marianne beside him. After all, who could possibly see *her* as a judge's wife?

Wife?

Where the hell had that come from?

Companion, then. Date. She was *so* not political material.

A fact that underscored the rationality of their original plan: Contract to sell the distillery plus a good time while they were negotiating equaled happy memories for both of them when they parted ways.

It was what they'd agreed, and it made sense.

And yet she couldn't deny that the thought of going their separate ways now left her feeling hollow. And the part where she watched another woman on his arm brought out some serious mean girl attitude.

Hell. She was definitely in trouble.

"Selma!" The eager voice yanked Selma away from her pity party, and she turned to find Elena grinning at her as she hurried forward, accompanied by an athletic woman with wild, curly hair and piercing blue eyes.

"Elena! Why are you here?"

"I'm schmoozing. I have an interview with the director of one of the historic preservation societies soon. Figured I should meet her socially first."

"Good plan." Elena was about to start a graduate

program in urban planning, and she was eager to get as much related experience as possible.

"What about you? Why are you here?"

"Easton had an extra ticket. I, um, I'm considering it a client perk."

"Easton Wallace?" the other woman asked. "I've been looking for him. I'm Hannah, by the way. Hannah Donovan."

"Hannah comes to The Fix sometimes. She's friends with Shelby. You met her once with Nolan, remember? Mr. April?"

Selma did. And she also remembered Hannah's name from the day she and Easton had worked in the conference room, and those ridiculous green monsters started up their conga line again. "I actually just saw him with another woman from his firm."

Hannah made a face. "Must be Marianne. I think Judge Coale only wants her as Easton's escort because she's too bland to be offensive to anybody."

Selma bit back a laugh, her estimation of this woman rising a bit. "How do you know Easton?"

Hannah waved a hand. "Oh, God, we go back forever. We were study buddies in law school, then mock trial partners. We dated for about seven seconds, but it didn't stick. We lost touch for about a year—I ended up dating a woman who was jealous of every ex-boyfriend—and then I moved to Austin to do in-house work and we reconnected."

The last bits of jealousy faded away.

"You know him because you're a client?"

Selma nodded. "He's negotiating the sale of my business."

Hannah's lips twitched. "If you say so."

"What?" Elena demanded.

Hannah looked at Selma. "I probably understated what good friends Easton and I are. To be honest, until Judge Coale started him on this path to be a judge, we were thinking about opening a firm together. I'm itching to be in the trenches. In-house pay is great, but the work can be monotonous."

Selma frowned, not sure she was following. Hannah, apparently, was a rambler, and Selma assumed that if they worked together, Easton would do the trial stuff and Hannah the behind the scenes law work.

"Right, sorry. My point is, we talk a lot. He's one of my closest friends, although with campaigning and his recent extracurricular activities, we haven't talked as much as we used to."

"Oh." Selma actually blushed. And blushing *really* wasn't like her. "What exactly has he told you?"

Hannah lifted a shoulder. "Nothing embarrassing. But I'm happy for him. It's clear he really likes you. Sorry it has to be so clandestine. Politics are stupid."

"That's for sure," Selma said.

Beside them, Elena looked from one to the other. "What the *hell* are you two talking about?"

"I'm fucking Easton," Selma said, choosing her words intentionally because it was so much fun to shock Elena. "But keep it a secret, okay?"

"But you're leaving for Scotland soon!"

"Maybe he's my grand send-off," Selma said, although the words tasted bitter on her tongue. "Either way, we're having fun."

"Speak of the devil," Hannah said, as Easton approached.

"You three look like you're getting into mischief."

"Always," Hannah said, as Selma's phone chirped, the tone signaling that it was Matthew.

She pulled it out, glanced at the screen, and went cold.

911.

"Excuse me." She stepped away, her heart pounding as she called her brother.

"Dad's had a heart attack," he said without preamble. Hell, she hadn't even heard the phone ring.

"Oh, God. Is he—"

"Fine. Stable. He's in a hospital in China. Mom says they're taking care of him. She tried to call you, too, but said it kept disconnecting."

"Are they coming home? Can I call her?"

"You can try. She said she'd email you when she had a moment. As for coming home, they're going to take a cruise back. She says it'll force Dad to rest."

Selma closed her eyes and nodded. When she opened them again, the women and Easton were looking at her with concern. "It's my dad. He's fine, but he had a heart attack." She aimed a thin smile at Easton. "Thank you for the ticket. I loved seeing the animals. But if you don't mind, I think I'm going to go home. I feel a little raw."

A thousand emotions seemed to shift over his face, and she knew that whatever he wanted to say, he couldn't in public. Right then, she didn't even care. She felt numb, and after she said her goodbyes, she drove home on autopilot, then curled up on her couch without even being certain how she managed to get inside.

She dozed for a few hours, then checked her email. As promised, her mother had sent an email updating her on her dad's status, which, thankfully, wasn't too scary. Honestly, it was the part her mother had tagged on at the end that made Selma's nerves twitch.

Sweetie, I know you're tired of hearing the same song from me, but I have to say it to you one more time—please stop playing Hopscotch through your life. I'm afraid that this close call with your father will push you the opposite direction. That you will imagine the pain of losing him and once again push everyone close in your life away simply so that you will have done it to them before they do it to you. You think I don't see that, but I do. I'm your mother, yes, but I had the benefit of watching you at first with a stranger's eyes. And I see you better than you think I do. And I love you for everything I see, but it worries me as well.

I want you to be happy and settled, but settled doesn't mean that you can't still travel and have fun. I want your life to be exciting and memorable. But don't hop about so much that you only land on the mountaintops. Take time to explore the ground beneath you. Live your life, Selma. Don't just bounce through it. Take time to love and to learn. I promise you, any pain that comes with it is a small price to pay for being connected.

I love you always and Dad and I will see you when we make port in the US. Until then, think of us sunning and relaxing on the deck of a ship. And also think about what I've said.

Much love and kisses forever,

Mom

SELMA TRIED to read the email twice, but with the tears filling her eyes, she couldn't. Instead, she hugged her phone close and closed her eyes, willing sleep—only to sit bolt upright when she felt a hand on her shoulder.

"I'm sorry." Easton's voice washed over her. "You left your door unlocked."

She sat up, groggy, and realized she'd been dozing. "What time is it? The benefit's already over?"

"I left early. I would have been here sooner, but I didn't know your address. I had to swing by the office and look it up."

"Home sweet home," she said, indicating the efficiency apartment that took up part of the distillery's second floor. She frowned. "You left early?"

"I was worried about you."

"Oh." The words warmed her, pleasing her more than she'd expected. "Who is Marianne to you?" She blinked. She hadn't intended to ask that question.

"No one," he said, his words giving credence to what Hannah had said. "My mentor thinks she's the perfect wingman for political events."

"She likes you. And not as a wingman."

He shook his head. "Not an issue."

"Maybe not for you. But I saw the look on her face."

"Again. Not an issue."

She ran her fingers through her hair. "What about Hannah?"

"Am I hearing jealousy?"

She met his eyes, took a deep breath, and said, "Yes."

"Oh." He actually flinched a bit in surprise. Not that she blamed him. Considering their deal, that pronouncement was definitely out of character. Hell, maybe her mother's words were getting to her more than Selma wanted them to.

"Good," he added, then grinned. "I think I like knowing you're jealous."

"Rat bastard," she said mildly. "Seriously, who is Hannah to you?"

"One of my best friends."

"That's what she said. I like corroborating

evidence." His chuckle washed over her and she pressed on. "Why aren't you opening your firm with her?"

"I'm doing the judicial thing."

"Again I ask, why?"

"A lot of reasons. The path makes sense, and I can help people."

"But it's not you. I mean, I've seen some interesting sides of you, and they're not particularly judicial. And as for helping people, don't judges deal with attorneys and not the actual clients?"

He said nothing, and when he did answer, his words were unexpected. And a bit unwelcome. "Why do you keep haggling over minor terms in the sale contract?"

"What? I'm not—"

"You are. We could have closed this deal days ago, but we keep going over the same ground. And I don't think it's just because you want to spend more time with me."

"I want the best deal."

"Maybe the best deal is no deal."

"Dammit, Easton, we're not doing the psychology game."

He lifted a brow. "Aren't we?"

"Fine." She stood up and thrust out her hand. "Truce?"

He tugged her toward him, then lifted her onto his lap and kissed her, the feel of his lips against hers and his body hot and hard beneath her settling her more than it should. "Truce," he murmured, then put his arms around her and hugged her against him.

For a moment, they stayed like that, with her clinging to him and soaking up his strength. After a moment, she pulled back, her eyes searching his and, thankfully, what she saw reflected there gave her the strength to say the next words. "I don't want to think that this is more than it is," she began. "I mean, we had a deal. But I want—"

"Fuck the deal." His voice was rough, sensual. "This is just you and me. No contracts. No rules. Our way, whatever we want that way to be."

"What way do you want?" she asked.

"I want to keep going. I want you in my bed. I want you in my life. Does that scare you?"

She licked her lips, then nodded.

"I'm sorry about that. But I don't think you're the kind of woman who runs from scary things."

A laugh bubbled out of her. "Oh, I think I do. Scary emotional things, anyway." She drew a breath, then cupped his cheek. "But I don't want to run from you."

"What do you want? Leaving aside selling the distillery, what is it you want to do?"

She cocked her head, considering the question. "I want to travel. See the world. I like exploring. I want to learn to paint. To read Greek. And I'd like to watch operas and Bollywood movies. I want to stomp grapes in France. And I don't want to wake up one day and realize I've lived my life with my nose in a balance sheet."

"And you don't think you can do all that and keep your distillery?"

She shrugged. "Certainly easier without."

"A lot of things are easy without. But it's lonelier, too."

Her mother's words seemed to echo in her head.

"Can I ask you a question?"

Once again, she laughed. "I thought you were."

He smirked. "How the hell did you break into my house?"

"Oh." The lightness evaporated. "Before the Herringtons adopted me and Matthew, we were in the system. I told you that, right? Well, before our birthmother abandoned us at the mall, she pretty much abandoned us at home. And we wouldn't have food for days and days."

"My God." The horror in his voice was clear.

"Yeah. It wasn't fun. But it was what it was. And so Matthew and I stole what we needed."

She spoke matter-of-factly, but when he took her hands in his, she knew he heard the pain underneath.

"He was never very good at security systems, but I could always manage to get around them. Honestly,

I hadn't tested my skill in a long time. Yours was tricky, but doable."

"Hmm. I'll get it upgraded." He paused, then, "Selma, I—"

She pressed her finger to her lips. "Don't even say it. No regrets. I've moved on."

"Have you?"

She turned away.

He hooked a finger under her chin and turned her head back to face him. "I don't like that you're moving to Scotland." His words made butterflies dance in her stomach. She'd told him her entire plan, of course, but so far they hadn't talked about it. "And I'm jealous as shit of this guy. Sean O'Reilly. Sounds like a bad guy in a Tom Clancy movie. You should steer clear."

She laughed, suddenly happier than she could remember being in a long time. Which made no sense. Except, of course, that it made all the sense in the world. "It's okay. He's engaged."

Easton's eyes narrowed. "All right then. Maybe he's okay." He sighed. "I don't know anymore."

"If he's okay?" She'd gotten confused along the way.

"What we're doing," he clarified. "Somewhere, I lost track of what we're doing."

"That's all right." She kissed him slow and deep. "We'll figure it out together."

Chapter Twelve

"JUST SO YOU KNOW, if you hurt my sister, I will kill you."

Easton sat on one of the padded benches in Matthew's gym and stared up at his friend. "I thought you were going to spot me?" They'd intended to go out for a drink, but except for very athletic sex, Easton hadn't gotten in a workout recently, so they'd decide to talk over weights and machines.

"I'll spot you while I interrogate you. Trust me. You want to give me the right answers."

"I have no intention of hurting your sister. What she does to herself, though, is out of my hands."

"What do you mean?"

"She doesn't want to sell the distillery. I just hope she realizes it before she makes a mistake."

Matthew seemed to study him. "Agreed. But what about you? Are you a mistake?"

Easton thought about the bullshit campaign. About how he'd let Marianne on his arm instead of the woman he was falling for, hard and fast. "I'm not," he said firmly. "But I've definitely made some mistakes. I'm going to correct them."

"How?"

"Not sure," Easton admitted. "But I like your sister. I think I might even love her." And wasn't that pretty damn scary? "So I promise you I'm going to figure it out."

In front of him, Matthew nodded. "Fair enough. Just know that if you do hurt her, don't come bitching to me if a heavy load of weights falls on your head one day."

Easton laughed. "We have a deal."

He spent a few more hours with Matthew, then headed over to see Selma, only to end up bereft when he didn't find her at home. He tracked her down, but she was with a group of girlfriends, and he hadn't crossed the line to being so needy he'd pull her away from her friends. Or, at least, he hadn't crossed the line to admitting he was that needy.

Unfortunately, that meant that he saw very little of her that week, because he was in trial in Waco, and drove up before dawn Monday morning. Selma, however, wasn't foiled by the distance; the woman made texting an art form. And all Easton had to do was remember to keep his phone away from his client and opposing counsel. No one else needed to see the naughty sexts they sent back and forth.

The trial was exhausting and brutal, which was a good thing. For one thing, he loved the excitement of being in front of the bench and thinking on his feet; that was something he'd definitely miss if he won the election.

On top of that, a perk of the intense concentration necessary for trial meant that he didn't have time to miss Selma or mourn their time apart.

But by the time he was finished with the final day's trial prep on Thursday night, he was definitely ready for some sexy texts. That, of course, was when she didn't send naughty pictures and raw words describing exactly what she intended to do when she saw him again. Instead, she texted him pictures of bats.

He called her on the phone within seconds. "Bats? I was hoping for breasts. Yours, actually."

The sound of her laughter made him smile. "Too bad for you. I'm working on a new logo for Bat Bourbon. What do you think of the middle image?"

He didn't bother looking. Just frowned at the phone. "Baby, what's going on with you?"

"Excuse me?"

"Branding isn't your concern anymore. Or it won't be after you sign."

"Oh. I know. I'm just fooling around. Besides, it's kind of my legacy. I should go out with the company and brand looking exactly like I want them too, right?"

Wrong.

But what he said was, "What are you afraid of?"

"Excuse me?"

"That if you keep the distillery you'll be trapped? There are no bars. That it might fail later so you should sell it now? It won't, and even if it does, you'll survive. That you'll be bored? You won't be. You could find something fascinating in a sea of asphalt. That's just the kind of person you are."

"Easton—"

"That you'll be alone?" He heard her sharp intake of breath. "You won't be."

"You can't promise that."

He hesitated, then closed his eyes. "Yeah. I think I can."

"I—" Her voice hitched.

"Come with me on Saturday to the event at the Children's Museum."

"What?"

"As my date."

"But—"

"I want you with me. I want us together."

She stayed silent.

"You told me once that you understood what it was like to have the world ripped out from under you," he said. "And I know the story behind *please.* Maybe it's time you stop being afraid, Selma. Say yes, and come with me."

For a moment, there was silence. Then he heard her soft, breathy, "Yes," followed by the click of the call disconnecting.

SELMA DIALED the country code for Scotland, then put her phone down.

Five minutes later, she picked it up again. This time, she got all the way through Sean's number before she slid the phone away.

The next time—an hour later after she'd showered —she forced herself to dial the full number and press the little handset icon.

She heard the weird ring that signified that it wasn't a US call, then tightened her grip so she wouldn't be tempted to hang up again.

A click, a yawn, and then a sleepy voice. "Selma?"

Damn. She hadn't factored in the time change.

"I'm sorry to wake you. I just—I wanted to talk to you soon. So you were in the loop."

"There's a loop?"

She smiled. The odd question coupled with his sexy Scottish voice crossed the line into funny.

"It's just that I—well, I won't be coming after all. I'm sorry if that leaves you in a lurch."

"Yeah?" Another yawn, followed by a soft, *it's okay, love, go back to sleep,* and when he came back on, he sounded more human. "What's up?"

"I just—well, honestly, there's a guy. No, that's not it." She shook her head. "It's Free-Tail. I'm not ready to give it up."

She closed her eyes and waited for him to lose his temper. She knew he'd been counting on her help. He'd even arranged a flat for her to lease.

A moment passed, then another. Then finally, he said, "If I were you, I couldn't walk away either."

"You're not mad?"

"Nah. Disappointed I won't be seeing you, but come make a trip when you can."

Relief flooded through her, and for the first time she was not only certain she'd done the right thing, but she felt one hundred percent comfortable with a longterm decision.

"I will."

"And Selma? If there is a guy in the picture, bring him, too. I want to meet the man who finally got under your skin."

HE HAD GOTTEN under her skin, Selma realized. And the most significant evidence was that she was standing in Elena's bedroom getting dressed for the Children's Museum function.

Since Easton had some sort of board meeting before the event, she was meeting him there. And she wanted him to know—not just through her words—that she'd made a decision. About her work, and her life.

Because frankly, she didn't want to see Marianne on

his arm anymore. She wanted that job, and she considered today an audition.

And none of her friends dressed as classy as Elena.

"It's a knockoff," Elena said. "But it's a good one."

"Chanel?"

"Classic," Elena said, holding the pale pink suit. "And you can match it with pearls and a silk blouse."

Selma looked at the conservative outfit dubiously, then reminded herself why she was doing this. She wanted to be a woman he didn't hesitate to show off.

But underneath the damn thing, she was wearing her thong.

"We can cover your wrist tattoo with makeup. And a quick rinse will put your hair all to black. We can style it close to your face. Classic makeup and then stunning shoes and you're all set."

"Shoes?" She hadn't thought to bring any.

"We're the same size. I've got you covered."

An hour later, Elena's words proved true. Selma

hardly recognized herself as she stood in front of the mirror decked out in a conservative but classic suit, a scoop neck silk blouse paired with a choker of pearls—fake, but decent quality. Her hair was styled with curls worn close to her scalp, giving her a little bit of a flapper look.

The shoes were kickass. Only three-inch heels, but the material was almost iridescent and it reflected the color of the dress.

As for her makeup, Selma had never worn so little, but she had to admit her eyes looked good. And the shade of lipstick was flattering, too.

"I think you're ready," Elena said. "Go get him, Tiger."

Laughing, Selma hugged her friend, then went outside to catch an Uber to the museum. Elena was living with her parents both to save money and to get to know her dad and her half-brother better, and that meant that they were too far away to walk.

Since Selma fully intended to go home with Easton, she'd taken an Uber to the house as well.

The ride downtown was quick, and Selma barely had

time to pull herself together before the car stopped in front of the museum and she found herself standing on the sidewalk with a bad case of nerves.

What if Easton felt differently? She was assuming he wanted something more permanent between them—and that her presenting herself conservatively in public would be a good idea.

But what if he hadn't really meant what he'd said? What if despite everything, he wanted to just keep going on as fuck buddies?

Honestly, the possibility was too depressing to consider. A fact that only confirmed to Selma how far gone she was for the man. Because not too long ago, she would have run from anyone who suggested anything more than random, no-strings sex.

Yet here she was, afraid that he didn't want to commit.

She wasn't sure if she should laugh or cry. Probably better not to do either considering the amount of mascara Elena had put on her lashes.

"Now or never," she murmured to herself, then

smiled at a passing stranger who gave her a curious look.

She entered the museum, was given directions to the event, and headed that way.

She saw him immediately. He stood at the far end of an open area lined with science exhibits. He looked like a celebrity in his suit, his chin lifted confidently, his gaze taking in all of the people around him. She wasn't convinced he wanted to be a judge, but in that moment she knew he had it in him to be elected.

Then he looked up, and his gaze landed right on her. And in that moment, all the air was sucked from the room. There was nothing left but him and her. She felt like Maria in the dance scene in *West Side Story* where everything faded away except her and Tony.

Hopefully her story and Easton's would have a much happier ending.

She stood transfixed as he moved to her and didn't breathe until he took her hands in his. "You look stunning. Hell, it's even more sexy knowing that under that suit you're hiding all those tats. Not to mention what I'm sure is some very sexy lingerie."

She smiled so wide that it hurt. "True. And thank you."

His eyes roamed over her for a few more minutes, then he shook his head, seeming to clear it. "Come on, I'll introduce you around. Judge Coale is here. I'd like you to meet him."

The butterflies that had kicked up a storm in response to that announcement wouldn't let her agree aloud, but she nodded, and they walked hand in hand to a distinguished octogenarian who held court by a pendulum. He paused as Easton approached, his smile as paternal as if Easton were his son.

"Judge Coale, I'd like you to meet my date, Selma Herrington, the owner of Austin Free-Tail Distillery."

"My dear, it's wonderful to meet you." The judge's grip was surprisingly strong, and it was clear to Selma why he'd been successful in politics. By the time they left she was not only charmed, but had no idea at all what the man thought of her. He was completely impossible to read.

"There are a few other folks I want you to meet,"

Easton began, but she cut him off with a hand to his arm.

"I want to, but I need to tell you something first."

He led her toward a hallway that appeared to lead to public meeting rooms. "What is it?"

She swallowed. "I want to cancel the deal. I don't want to sell. I don't want to go to Scotland."

"I see."

"No," she said. "I'm not sure you do." She drew in a breath. "What I do want, is you."

A muscle twitched in his cheek, but otherwise, he didn't react. For a moment, she feared that she'd gotten everything wrong. That this was not good news to him, and that she'd just made a huge fool of herself.

Then he grabbed her hand, squeezing hard, and hurried down the hall as if they were escaping a fire. He pushed open one of the meeting room doors, kicked it shut, then slammed her up against the wall.

"Christ, Selma, do you have any idea what you do to me?"

"I—"

"What hearing you say that does to me? Seeing you dressed like this, knowing you're doing it for me. I mean, pearls. Baby, you're amazing."

His fingers closed over the pearls. He was breathing hard. So was she.

"So this is good? You're not—"

"I'm not anything but turned on. You couldn't have said anything better to me. Christ, when I get you home tonight…"

"Yes," she murmured as his hand cupped her breast.

And then, without warning, he said, "Fuck it." Using the pearls as leverage, he pulled her toward him. The cheap strand snapped, sending white beads everywhere, but she didn't care.

"Ignore it," she said, pulling his head closer and opening her mouth to his. He kissed her hard. Tongue and teeth and the taste of blood. His hands seemed to be everywhere. Her hands, her thighs. She realized he had her skirt up, his hand between her legs, his body pressed close.

"Now," he said. "I have to be inside you now."

"Easton, the party."

"The door's locked. We're fine."

She moaned as his fingers slid into her.

"The door's not—"

And then the door burst open.

He tugged his hand free and moved to shield her with his body even as she blinked from the camera flashes that suddenly and completely filled the room.

Chapter Thirteen

"I'M SO DAMN SORRY. So goddamn, *fucking* sorry."

Easton had been repeating the same thing over and over again all the way back to her distillery. She knew he was mortified, but she was all right. She wished he'd just talk to her instead of apologizing repeatedly.

"I lost my head," he said. "And now your reputation, my reputation." He pulled in behind her building, then slammed his palm against the steering wheel. "*Shit.*"

"Just come on up. We're tired. We'll sleep. We'll talk about it more in the morning."

He shook his head. "And then Marianne standing right there with the press, telling them that I was some asshole who couldn't control himself, and you're just some skank who's been following me around until I finally gave in."

She tensed. When Marianne had blurted that out as Selma had been jerking her clothes back in place, she'd had to use all of her self-control not to throw a shoe at the bitch.

"She's just jealous that you're the candidate and she's not."

"I'm not the candidate anymore, though, am I? One night with you actually as my date, and it all goes to fucking hell."

She froze. She just absolutely froze. "What did you say?"

He dragged his hands through his hair. "I'm just angry."

"Do *not* blame this on me. I came there wearing what I was supposed to wear and acting the way I was supposed to act. You're the one who decided a fast fuck in the back room sounded like a good idea."

"And who do you think planted that seed in my head? The first time I see you after a decade you're groping me at my office or The Fix or in the ladies room of The Winston."

She swallowed, anger boiling so hot she thought her hair might catch on fire. She opened her door. It was the only thing she could manage. "Goodnight, Easton," she said as she got out, her eyes held wide as she fought tears.

He leaned toward her, calling something as she slammed the door shut. It might have been *I'm sorry*. But she couldn't hear him. And by that time, honestly, it was too little, too late.

"WOW," Hannah said as she peered at Easton's face. "That's quite a shiner. When did you get that?"

"Yesterday," he said. They were eating sandwiches in her office at the financial management firm where she worked. For the time being, he was avoiding eating out.

"Who?"

"That would be Matthew."

Hannah's eyes went wide. "Selma's brother?"

"I asked him to intervene for me with Selma. He punched me. Guess I know where he stands."

"Hmmm." She leaned back in her chair. "And where do *you* stand?"

"Well, I'm out of the judicial race. Judge Coale is officially disappointed in me."

"I'm sorry. I know you two were close."

"We've smoothed it over. I explained that I'm in love with her." Just saying the words made him feel good. What would make him feel better is if he could say them to her.

Selma, however, was avoiding him. And he'd never felt more useless, horrible, and generally downtrodden in his life.

Hannah sat up straighter. "Oh?"

"Not that it matters. She doesn't know how I feel. I was hoping Matthew could help me out. No such luck."

"So you haven't told her yet?"

"After what I said the night of the museum party,

saying I love you in an email or a voice mail or a text seems tacky. And I haven't managed to talk to her in person since she stormed out of my car. Honestly, I deserve the smackdown. I know I do. I just want the chance to talk to her. Got any ideas?"

At this point he was open to most anything. He missed her so much his chest ached. And he was kicking himself on a daily basis for saying such stupid things to her. He'd been mad at himself, and he'd taken it out on her.

Honestly, though, he should have been thanking her. Because the very best thing that had come out of the whole fiasco was the certainty that he didn't want to be a judge.

He wanted what he'd always wanted—what he'd been sidetracked from. He wanted a small firm where he dealt with real people.

Hopefully, those real people wouldn't mind that he'd been caught feeling up his girlfriend in public. *Idiot.*

"So what are you doing now? Did you lose your job?"

"Remarkably, no. They're keeping me on conditionally. I think they're uncertain whether my notoriety will draw clients or push them away."

"And you're okay with that?"

"What choice do I have?"

She smiled wide and pointed to herself. "Offer still stands."

His brows rose. "You don't want to. I'm pretty sure at this point I'm toxic."

"The hell you are. This will blow over. I promise you. Especially once you and the supposed skank are back together."

"*If*," he said. "I'm honestly not sure we'll ever get back together." The thought made his gut clench. Surely he'd find a way…

"From what you've told me, you haven't tried groveling."

He cocked his head, trying to read her mind. "What are you thinking?"

"That tomorrow's Wednesday," she said. "And I have an idea."

Chapter Fourteen

THE WEDNESDAY NIGHT of the Mr. September contest at The Fix on Sixth was even more crowded than usual, probably because Hannah had leaked to the press that Easton was going to be there. She'd also told Selma that she should come, and now Selma sat on a bar stool, wondering if this was a good idea or a very, very bad one. Not because Easton apparently wanted to talk to her desperately, but because the press kept surreptitiously snapping pictures of her.

"I thought you said he wanted to talk to me," she said to Hannah as they sipped Loaded Coronas.

"He does. He will." She leaned closer. "Are you any less mad at him?"

Selma sighed. "I don't know. He hurt my feelings— a lot. But he was partly right. I did do stupid things early on. We could have just as easily gotten caught the time I made him go down on me in the ladies' room at The Winston."

Hannah's eyes widened. "You do know that I can't un-hear that, right?"

"Hey, he's going to be your law partner. That's like a marriage, right?"

Hannah grinned. "You *are* less mad at him."

"I just—he blamed me. And it didn't feel good."

"I promise you, he feels terrible about that. He knows it was a dick move. He has no defense."

"Then what does he want to talk about?"

But Hannah only lifted her shoulder, which meant that Selma had to wait until she found out. And Selma wasn't in the mood to wait.

She wanted to talk to Easton.

The truth was, as furious as she'd been after the museum, the bottom line was that he'd gotten into her heart. She wanted him. Hell, she needed him. And she was more than ready to talk to him.

So where the hell was he?

The music started for the contest, and she cast her eyes around, looking for him in the audience. But he was nowhere to be found, so she sighed and settled in to watch, figuring she'd find him after when the crowd thinned out.

The contest positively dragged for her, however, because she wasn't interested. And when the final contestant came on stage, she leaned over and told Hannah that she was going to the ladies' room.

"No, wait."

"I really need to get out of this crowd." She slipped off her stool before Hannah could protest again, and was fighting her way to the back when the emcee, Beverly Martin, told the crowd to "give it up for our unexpected bonus contestant—Easton Wallace!"

She froze by the hall, then turned to see Easton strutting down the red carpet, looking more than a little sheepish.

He took the mic from Beverly, then looked out at the crowd. "Those of you who don't know me will probably Google my name after this announcement, but here it is. First, I'm officially pulling my name from any judicial races. Not just because of the recent scandal, but because it's not my dream. I got caught up in the frenzy and forgot to think about my real goals."

The crowd had gone silent. Selma stepped closer.

"I've always been a little scared to follow my dream. What I wanted to do seemed impulsive. But I've learned a bit about not being scared of making a leap. Not everything I do needs to follow lockstep on the corporate or legal path. And every once in a while I need to look around and see if I'm living the life I want … or someone else's that I put on like a suit jacket. Because even if it fits perfectly, that's not my jacket."

He cleared his throat and searched the crowd—and the instant his eyes found hers, she felt the heat of connection. "I also learned that sometimes you need to make the grand gesture. To really throw yourself out there. Selma, baby, this is for you."

And then, with the audience howling and clapping, he yanked off his slacks—obviously the velcro kind that strippers wear—then repeated the process with his shirt until he was standing there in only his loafers and briefs.

She clapped her hand over her mouth so hard she almost bruised her lips, and as she tried to hold back laughter, she saw a dark line on his chest, but couldn't make out what it was from so far away.

"I walked away from one election today. Now I'm going to walk away from this one. Vote for me, don't vote for me. I'm done campaigning. There's only one person I want to win over. And I'm going to go see if I can do that right now. And I hope that this is some tiny bit of proof that I mean what I say."

He pointed to the dark line, and camera flashes popped.

"I had it done today. It's a tattoo. It says *please*."

Her heart skipped a beat, and she gasped.

"I got it for you, Selma. It means this—please let her be the one. And please let it last."

He inclined his head, and as the crowd started to applaud, he walked back down the red carpet, grabbing a duffel bag from next to the wall before turning toward her.

She met his eyes, nodded, then walked into the hallway, her heart pounding in her chest.

"I should get dressed," he said when he found her by the shelves of paper products outside of Tyree's office.

She shook her head as she looked him up and down, fighting her smile. Then she stepped forward and put her hand on the tattoo. "Scandalous," she said.

"I'm so goddamn sorry."

The apology filled her, and she smiled.

"I was an idiot," he continued.

"Yeah, you were."

"But I have something going for me."

"What's that?" she asked.

"I'm a hard worker. And right now, my number one priority is you."

"Oh, really?" She forced herself not to smile. "How's that?"

"I'm going to convince you to stay with me. That you belong with me. That I'm a man who will never stop doing whatever I can to make you happy. To make every day together an adventure."

"Oh." She licked her lips, trying to stave off tears. "How are you going to do that?"

"Not sure, but I know I'll never stop trying."

"I like the sound of that."

"And there's one other thing," he said, then cupped her chin. "I love you, Selma Herrington."

Happiness flooded through her. "I love you, too," she said, then grinned as she bit her lower lip.

"What?"

She reached for the door to Tyree's office, then pushed it open. "I'm feeling a bit scandalous. You?"

His chuckle filled the hall. "Always," he said, then tugged her inside the room and shut the door.

This time, she noticed, he locked it.

Epilogue

MATTHEW WAS FILLING his plate with sliced brisket and potato salad when Hannah stepped up beside him, her mere proximity sending awareness coursing through him. She pressed her palm against his back, then leaned close, her manner so casual it almost seemed as if they really were dating.

She was good at deception, that was for sure. Matthew, however, was not. About the only thing he was managing to pull off successfully was an air of being head-over-heels for the woman who was his pretend fiancée. But since Hannah Donovan had mesmerized him from the first moment he'd met her, that really didn't strain his meager acting skills.

"Hey, stud," she said. "If you get the food, I'll get

the wine. I grabbed us a table near the band. And after the bride and groom do the first dance, we can go out on the floor, too. Less talking to people about our engagement if we're lost in each other's arms, right?"

He swallowed, imagining the feel of her against him during a slow dance. "Sounds good. I'll meet you at the table in a—"

"Oh, *hell*. Red alert." The harsh, almost scared, tone of her voice cut through him, making him want to hold her close and soothe her. "It's my dad."

His stomach curdled, his protective instincts now warring with a strong urge to just get the hell out of there.

But he couldn't. The man was the entire reason he and Hannah were at this wedding together. Why they were pretending to be engaged. Why she'd been looking at him all gooey-eyed for most of the evening, and he'd been diligently reminding himself that it was fake. All fake.

"Let's head over and talk to one of your friends," Matthew suggested.

"Too late. He's heading toward us. Dammit, I don't want to deal with him right now."

"You and me both." He hadn't had the pleasure of meeting Mr. Donovan yet, but he'd heard enough to already be wildly intimidated by the successful lawyer. Matthew knew his strengths, and he also knew that if Ernest Donovan wanted to discuss legal ideas, current events, or even great literature, Matthew was going to come across sounding like a goddamn idiot. *Shit.*

Why the hell had he said he'd do this? He didn't think fast on his feet. Words always escaped him.

"Quick," Hannah said. "If we're already talking about something, he won't ask us about the engagement. Um, the school voucher system everyone keeps talking about. I think the Legislature's going to look at it again for Texas this year. What do you think about that?"

Terror ripped through him. He didn't have a clue about vouchers, and since he had no kids, he didn't much care at the moment, either. Anything he said would reveal to Hannah that he was a clueless fool, and that was one thing he didn't want to be.

"Or you pick a topic," she said urgently. "Just talk. He's almost here."

But there was no topic. There was nothing for him to do.

Nothing except one thing.

He left the brisket on the table, pulled her roughly against him, and kissed her.

For a moment, she was stiff with shock. Then she melted against him, her mouth opening under his.

He sighed, lost in the feel of her. Because *this* felt right. Not overwhelming like the rest of it. *This*— the woman, the kiss, the pressure of their bodies —*this* was the way it should be.

And for one brief, delicious moment, Matthew knew what heaven felt like.

Too bad he was about to get kicked right back down to earth again.

Are you eager to learn which Man of the Month book features which sexy hero? Here's a handy list!

Down On Me - meet Reece
Hold On Tight - meet Spencer
Need You Now - meet Cameron
Start Me Up - meet Nolan
Get It On - meet Tyree
In Your Eyes - meet Parker
Turn Me On - meet Derek
Shake It Up - meet Landon
All Night Long - meet Easton
In Too Deep - meet Matthew
Light My Fire - meet Griffin
Walk The Line - meet Brent
&
Bar Bites: A Man of the Month Cookbook

Down On Me excerpt

Did you miss book one in the Man of the Month series? Here's an excerpt from Down On Me!

Chapter One

Reece Walker ran his palms over the slick, soapy ass of the woman in his arms and knew that he was going straight to hell.

Not because he'd slept with a woman he barely knew. Not because he'd enticed her into bed with a series of well-timed bourbons and particularly inventive half-truths. Not even because he'd lied to his best friend Brent about why Reece couldn't drive with him to the airport to pick up Jenna, the third player in their trifecta of lifelong friendship.

No, Reece was staring at the fiery pit because he was a lame, horny asshole without the balls to tell the naked beauty standing in the shower with him that she wasn't the woman he'd been thinking about for the last four hours.

And if that wasn't one of the pathways to hell, it damn sure ought to be.

He let out a sigh of frustration, and Megan tilted her head, one eyebrow rising in question as she slid her hand down to stroke his cock, which was demonstrating no guilt whatsoever about the whole going to hell issue. "Am I boring you?"

"Hardly." That, at least, was the truth. He felt like a prick, yes. But he was a well-satisfied one. "I was just thinking that you're beautiful."

She smiled, looking both shy and pleased—and Reece felt even more like a heel. What the devil was wrong with him? She *was* beautiful. And hot and funny and easy to talk to. Not to mention good in bed.

But she wasn't Jenna, which was a ridiculous comparison. Because Megan qualified as fair game, whereas Jenna was one of his two best friends. She trusted him. Loved him. And despite the way his cock perked up at the thought of doing all sorts of delicious things with her in bed, Reece knew damn well that would never happen. No way was he risking their friendship. Besides, Jenna didn't love him like that. Never had, never would.

And that—plus about a billion more reasons—meant that Jenna was entirely off-limits.

Too bad his vivid imagination hadn't yet gotten the memo.

Fuck it.

He tightened his grip, squeezing Megan's perfect rear. "Forget the shower," he murmured. "I'm taking you back to bed." He needed this. Wild. Hot. Demanding. And dirty enough to keep him from thinking.

Hell, he'd scorch the earth if that's what it took to burn Jenna from his mind—and he'd leave Megan limp, whimpering, and very, very satisfied. His guilt. Her pleasure. At least it would be a win for one of them.

And who knows? Maybe he'd manage to fuck the fantasies of his best friend right out of his head.

It didn't work.

Reece sprawled on his back, eyes closed, as Megan's gentle fingers traced the intricate outline of the tattoos inked across his pecs and down his arms. Her touch was warm and tender, in stark contrast to the way he'd just fucked her—a little too wild, a little too hard, as if he were fighting a battle, not making love.

Well, that was true, wasn't it?

But it was a battle he'd lost. Victory would have brought oblivion. Yet here he was, a naked woman beside him, and his thoughts still on Jenna, as wild and intense and impossible as they'd been since that night eight months ago when the earth had shifted beneath him, and he'd let himself look at her as a woman and not as a friend.

One breathtaking, transformative night, and Jenna didn't even realize it. And he'd be damned if he'd ever let her figure it out.

Beside him, Megan continued her exploration, one fingertip tracing the outline of a star. "No names? No wife or girlfriend's initials hidden in the design?"

He turned his head sharply, and she burst out laughing.

"Oh, don't look at me like that." She pulled the sheet up to cover her breasts as she rose to her knees beside him. "I'm just making conversation. No hidden agenda at all. Believe me, the last thing I'm interested in is a relationship." She scooted away, then sat on the edge of the bed, giving him an enticing view of her bare back. "I don't even do overnights."

As if to prove her point, she bent over, grabbed her bra off the floor, and started getting dressed.

"Then that's one more thing we have in common." He pushed himself up, rested his back against the headboard, and enjoyed the view as she wiggled into her jeans.

"Good," she said, with such force that he knew she meant it, and for a moment he wondered what had soured her on relationships.

As for himself, he hadn't soured so much as fizzled. He'd had a few serious girlfriends over the years, but it never worked out. No matter how good it started, invariably the relationship crumbled. Eventually, he had to acknowledge that he simply wasn't relationship material. But that didn't mean he was a monk, the last eight months notwithstanding.

She put on her blouse and glanced around, then slipped her feet into her shoes. Taking the hint, he got up and pulled on his jeans and T-shirt. "Yes?" he asked, noticing the way she was eying him speculatively.

"The truth is, I was starting to think you might be in a relationship."

"What? Why?"

She shrugged. "You were so quiet there for a while, I wondered if maybe I'd misjudged you. I thought you might be married and feeling guilty."

Guilty.

The word rattled around in his head, and he groaned. "Yeah, you could say that."

"Oh, *hell*. Seriously?"

"No," he said hurriedly. "Not that. I'm not cheating on my non-existent wife. I wouldn't. Not ever." Not in small part because Reece wouldn't ever have a wife since he thought the institution of marriage was a crock, but he didn't see the need to explain that to Megan.

"But as for guilt?" he continued. "Yeah, tonight I've got that in spades."

She relaxed slightly. "Hmm. Well, sorry about the guilt, but I'm glad about the rest. I have rules, and I consider myself a good judge of character. It makes me cranky when I'm wrong."

"Wouldn't want to make you cranky."

"Oh, you really wouldn't. I can be a total bitch." She sat on the edge of the bed and watched as he tugged on his boots. "But if you're not hiding a wife in your attic, what are you feeling guilty about? I assure you, if it has anything to do with my satisfaction, you needn't feel guilty at all." She flashed a mischievous grin, and he couldn't help but smile back. He hadn't invited a woman into his bed for eight long months. At least he'd had the good fortune to pick one he actually liked.

"It's just that I'm a crappy friend," he admitted.

"I doubt that's true."

"Oh, it is," he assured her as he tucked his wallet into his back pocket. The irony, of course, was that as far as Jenna knew, he was an excellent friend. The best. One of her two pseudo-brothers with whom she'd sworn a blood oath the summer after sixth grade, almost twenty years ago.

From Jenna's perspective, Reece was at least as good as Brent, even if the latter scored bonus points because he was picking Jenna up at the airport while Reece was trying to fuck his personal demons into oblivion. Trying anything, in fact, that would exorcise the memory of how she'd clung to him that night, her curves enticing and her breath intoxicating, and not just because of the scent of too much alcohol.

She'd trusted him to be the white knight, her noble rescuer, and all he'd been able to think about was the feel of her body, soft and warm against his, as he carried her up the stairs to her apartment.

A wild craving had hit him that night, like a tidal wave of emotion crashing over him, washing away the outer shell of friendship and leaving nothing but raw desire and a longing so potent it nearly brought him to his knees.

It had taken all his strength to keep his distance when the only thing he'd wanted was to cover every inch of her naked body with kisses. To stroke her skin and watch her writhe with pleasure.

He'd won a hard-fought battle when he reined in his desire that night. But his victory wasn't without its wounds. She'd pierced his heart when she'd drifted to sleep in his arms, whispering that she loved him—and he knew that she meant it only as a friend.

More than that, he knew that he was the biggest asshole to ever walk the earth.

Thankfully, Jenna remembered nothing of that night. The liquor had stolen her memories, leaving her with a monster hangover, and him with a Jenna-shaped hole in his heart.

"Well?" Megan pressed. "Are you going to tell me? Or do I have to guess?"

"I blew off a friend."

"Yeah? That probably won't score you points in the Friend of the Year competition, but it doesn't sound too dire. Unless you were the best man and blew off the wedding? Left someone stranded at the side of the road somewhere in West Texas? Or promised to feed their cat and totally forgot? Oh, God. Please tell me you didn't kill Fluffy."

He bit back a laugh, feeling slightly better. "A friend came in tonight, and I feel like a complete shit for not meeting her plane."

"Well, there are taxis. And I assume she's an adult?"

"She is, and another friend is there to pick her up."

"I see," she said, and the way she slowly nodded suggested that she saw too much. "I'm guessing that *friend* means *girlfriend*? Or, no. You wouldn't do that. So she must be an ex."

"Really not," he assured her. "Just a friend. Lifelong, since sixth grade."

"Oh, I get it. Longtime friend. High expectations. She's going to be pissed."

"Nah. She's cool. Besides, she knows I usually work nights."

"Then what's the problem?"

He ran his hand over his shaved head, the bristles from the day's growth like sandpaper against his palm. "Hell if I know," he lied, then forced a smile, because whether his problem was guilt or lust or just plain stupidity, she hardly deserved to be on the receiving end of his bullshit.

He rattled his car keys. "How about I buy you one last drink before I take you home?"

"You're sure you don't mind a working drink?" Reece asked as he helped Megan out of his cherished baby blue vintage Chevy pickup. "Normally I wouldn't take you to my job, but we just hired a new bar back, and I want to see how it's going."

He'd snagged one of the coveted parking spots on Sixth Street, about a block down from The Fix, and he glanced automatically toward the bar, the glow from the windows relaxing him. He didn't own the place, but it was like a second home to him and had been for one hell of a long time.

"There's a new guy in training, and you're not there? I thought you told me you were the manager?"

"I did, and I am, but Tyree's there. The owner, I mean. He's always on site when someone new is starting. Says it's his job, not mine. Besides,

Sunday's my day off, and Tyree's a stickler for keeping to the schedule."

"Okay, but why are you going then?"

"Honestly? The new guy's my cousin. He'll probably give me shit for checking in on him, but old habits die hard." Michael had been almost four when Vincent died, and the loss of his dad hit him hard. At sixteen, Reece had tried to be stoic, but Uncle Vincent had been like a second father to him, and he'd always thought of Mike as more brother than cousin. Either way, from that day on, he'd made it his job to watch out for the kid.

"Nah, he'll appreciate it," Megan said. "I've got a little sister, and she gripes when I check up on her, but it's all for show. She likes knowing I have her back. And as for getting a drink where you work, I don't mind at all."

As a general rule, late nights on Sunday were dead, both in the bar and on Sixth Street, the popular downtown Austin street that had been a focal point of the city's nightlife for decades. Tonight was no exception. At half-past one in the morning, the street was mostly deserted. Just a few cars moving slowly, their headlights shining toward the west, and a smattering of couples, stumbling and laughing. Probably tourists on their way back to one of the downtown hotels.

It was late April, though, and the spring weather was drawing both locals and tourists. Soon, the area —and the bar—would be bursting at the seams. Even on a slow Sunday night.

Situated just a few blocks down from Congress Avenue, the main downtown artery, The Fix on Sixth attracted a healthy mix of tourists and locals. The bar had existed in one form or another for decades, becoming a local staple, albeit one that had been falling deeper and deeper into disrepair until Tyree had bought the place six years ago and started it on much-needed life support.

"You've never been here before?" Reece asked as he paused in front of the oak and glass doors etched with the bar's familiar logo.

"I only moved downtown last month. I was in Los Angeles before."

The words hit Reece with unexpected force. Jenna had been in LA, and a wave of both longing and regret crashed over him. He should have gone with Brent. What the hell kind of friend was he, punishing Jenna because he couldn't control his own damn libido?

With effort, he forced the thoughts back. He'd already beaten that horse to death.

"Come on," he said, sliding one arm around her shoulder and pulling open the door with his other. "You're going to love it."

He led her inside, breathing in the familiar mix of alcohol, southern cooking, and something indiscernible he liked to think of as the scent of a damn good time. As he expected, the place was mostly empty. There was no live music on Sunday nights, and at less than an hour to closing, there were only three customers in the front room.

"Megan, meet Cameron," Reece said, pulling out a stool for her as he nodded to the bartender in introduction. Down the bar, he saw Griffin Draper, a regular, lift his head, his face obscured by his hoodie, but his attention on Megan as she chatted with Cam about the house wines.

Reece nodded hello, but Griffin turned back to his notebook so smoothly and nonchalantly that Reece wondered if maybe he'd just been staring into space, thinking, and hadn't seen Reece or Megan at all. That was probably the case, actually. Griff wrote a popular podcast that had been turned into an even more popular web series, and when he wasn't recording the dialogue, he was usually writing a script.

"So where's Mike? With Tyree?"

Cameron made a face, looking younger than his twenty-four years. "Tyree's gone."

"You're kidding. Did something happen with Mike?" His cousin was a responsible kid. Surely he hadn't somehow screwed up his first day on the job.

"No, Mike's great." Cam slid a Scotch in front of Reece. "Sharp, quick, hard worker. He went off the clock about an hour ago, though. So you just missed him."

"Tyree shortened his shift?"

Cam shrugged. "Guess so. Was he supposed to be on until closing?"

"Yeah." Reece frowned. "He was. Tyree say why he cut him loose?"

"No, but don't sweat it. Your cousin's fitting right in. Probably just because it's Sunday and slow. " He made a face. "And since Tyree followed him out, guess who's closing for the first time alone."

"So you're in the hot seat, huh? " Reece tried to sound casual. He was standing behind Megan's stool, but now he moved to lean against the bar, hoping his casual posture suggested that he wasn't worried at all. He was, but he didn't want Cam to realize it. Tyree didn't leave employees to close on their own. Not until he'd spent weeks training them.

"I told him I want the weekend assistant manager position. I'm guessing this is his way of seeing how I work under pressure."

"Probably," Reece agreed half-heartedly. "What did he say?"

"Honestly, not much. He took a call in the office, told Mike he could head home, then about fifteen minutes later said he needed to take off, too, and that I was the man for the night."

"Trouble?" Megan asked.

"No. Just chatting up my boy," Reece said, surprised at how casual his voice sounded. Because the scenario had trouble printed all over it. He just wasn't sure what kind of trouble.

He focused again on Cam. "What about the wait-staff?" Normally, Tiffany would be in the main bar taking care of the customers who sat at tables. "He didn't send them home, too, did he?"

"Oh, no," Cam said. "Tiffany and Aly are scheduled to be on until closing, and they're in the back with—"

But his last words were drowned out by a high-pitched squeal of "*You're here!*" and Reece looked up to find Jenna Montgomery—the woman he craved —barreling across the room and flinging herself into his arms.

Meet Damien Stark

Only his passion could set her free…

Release Me
Claim Me
Complete Me
Anchor Me
Lost With Me

Meet Damien Stark in Release Me, *book 1 of the wildly sensual series that's left millions of readers breathless …*

Chapter One

A cool ocean breeze caresses my bare shoulders,

and I shiver, wishing I'd taken my roommate's advice and brought a shawl with me tonight. I arrived in Los Angeles only four days ago, and I haven't yet adjusted to the concept of summer temperatures changing with the setting of the sun. In Dallas, June is hot, July is hotter, and August is hell.

Not so in California, at least not by the beach. LA Lesson Number One: Always carry a sweater if you'll be out after dark.

Of course, I could leave the balcony and go back inside to the party. Mingle with the millionaires. Chat up the celebrities. Gaze dutifully at the paintings. It is a gala art opening, after all, and my boss brought me here to meet and greet and charm and chat. Not to lust over the panorama that is coming alive in front of me. Bloodred clouds bursting against the pale orange sky. Blue-gray waves shimmering with dappled gold.

I press my hands against the balcony rail and lean forward, drawn to the intense, unreachable beauty of the setting sun. I regret that I didn't bring the battered Nikon I've had since high school. Not that it would have fit in my itty-bitty beaded purse. And a bulky camera bag paired with a little black dress is a big, fat fashion no-no.

But this is my very first Pacific Ocean sunset, and I'm determined to document the moment. I pull out my iPhone and snap a picture.

"Almost makes the paintings inside seem redundant, doesn't it?" I recognize the throaty, feminine voice and turn to face Evelyn Dodge, retired actress turned agent turned patron of the arts—and my hostess for the evening.

"I'm so sorry. I know I must look like a giddy tourist, but we don't have sunsets like this in Dallas."

"Don't apologize," she says. "I pay for that view every month when I write the mortgage check. It damn well better be spectacular."

I laugh, immediately more at ease.

"Hiding out?"

"Excuse me?"

"You're Carl's new assistant, right?" she asks, referring to my boss of three days.

"Nikki Fairchild."

"I remember now. Nikki from Texas." She looks me up and down, and I wonder if she's disappointed that I don't have big hair and cowboy boots. "So who does he want you to charm?"

"Charm?" I repeat, as if I don't know exactly what she means.

She cocks a single brow. "Honey, the man would rather walk on burning coals than come to an art show. He's fishing for investors and you're the bait." She makes a rough noise in the back of her throat. "Don't worry. I won't press you to tell me who. And I don't blame you for hiding out. Carl's brilliant, but he's a bit of a prick."

"It's the brilliant part I signed on for," I say, and she barks out a laugh.

The truth is that she's right about me being the bait. "Wear a cocktail dress," Carl had said. "Something flirty."

Seriously? I mean, *Seriously?*

I should have told him to wear his own damn cocktail dress. But I didn't. Because I want this job. I fought to get this job. Carl's company, C-Squared Technologies, successfully launched three web-based products in the last eighteen months. That track record had caught the industry's eye, and Carl had been hailed as a man to watch.

More important from my perspective, that meant he was a man to learn from, and I'd prepared for the job interview with an intensity bordering on obsession. Landing the position had been a huge coup for me. So what if he wanted me to wear something flirty? It was a small price to pay.

Shit.

"I need to get back to being the bait," I say.

"Oh, hell. Now I've gone and made you feel either guilty or self-conscious. Don't be. Let them get liquored up in there first. You catch more flies with alcohol anyway. Trust me. I know."

She's holding a pack of cigarettes, and now she taps one out, then extends the pack to me. I shake my head. I love the smell of tobacco—it reminds me of my grandfather—but actually inhaling the smoke does nothing for me.

"I'm too old and set in my ways to quit," she says. "But God forbid I smoke in my own damn house. I swear, the mob would burn me in effigy. You're not going to start lecturing me on the dangers of secondhand smoke, are you?"

"No," I promise.

"Then how about a light?"

I hold up the itty-bitty purse. "One lipstick, a credit card, my driver's license, and my phone."

"No condom?"

"I didn't think it was that kind of party," I say dryly.

"I knew I liked you." She glances around the balcony. "What the hell kind of party am I throwing if I don't even have one goddamn candle on one goddamn table? Well, fuck it." She puts the unlit cigarette to her mouth and inhales, her eyes closed and her expression rapturous. I can't help but like her. She wears hardly any makeup, in stark contrast to all the other women here tonight, myself included, and her dress is more of a caftan, the batik pattern as interesting as the woman herself.

She's what my mother would call a brassy broad—

loud, large, opinionated, and self-confident. My mother would hate her. I think she's awesome.

She drops the unlit cigarette onto the tile and grinds it with the toe of her shoe. Then she signals to one of the catering staff, a girl dressed all in black and carrying a tray of champagne glasses.

The girl fumbles for a minute with the sliding door that opens onto the balcony, and I imagine those flutes tumbling off, breaking against the hard tile, the scattered shards glittering like a wash of diamonds.

I picture myself bending to snatch up a broken stem. I see the raw edge cutting into the soft flesh at the base of my thumb as I squeeze. I watch myself clutching it tighter, drawing strength from the pain, the way some people might try to extract luck from a rabbit's foot.

The fantasy blurs with memory, jarring me with its potency. It's fast and powerful, and a little disturbing because I haven't needed the pain in a long time, and I don't understand why I'm thinking about it now, when I feel steady and in control.

I am fine, I think. *I am fine, I am fine, I am fine.*

"Take one, honey," Evelyn says easily, holding a flute out to me.

I hesitate, searching her face for signs that my mask has slipped and she's caught a glimpse of my rawness. But her face is clear and genial.

"No, don't you argue," she adds, misinterpreting my hesitation. "I bought a dozen cases and I hate to see good alcohol go to waste. Hell no," she adds when the girl tries to hand her a flute. "I hate the stuff. Get me a vodka. Straight up. Chilled. Four olives. Hurry up, now. Do you want me to dry up like a leaf and float away?"

The girl shakes her head, looking a bit like a twitchy, frightened rabbit. Possibly one that had sacrificed his foot for someone else's good luck.

Evelyn's attention returns to me. "So how do you like LA? What have you seen? Where have you been? Have you bought a map of the stars yet? Dear God, tell me you're not getting sucked into all that tourist bullshit."

"Mostly I've seen miles of freeway and the inside of my apartment."

"Well, that's just sad. Makes me even more glad

that Carl dragged your skinny ass all the way out here tonight."

I've put on fifteen welcome pounds since the years when my mother monitored every tiny thing that went in my mouth, and while I'm perfectly happy with my size-eight ass, I wouldn't describe it as skinny. I know Evelyn means it as a compliment, though, and so I smile. "I'm glad he brought me, too. The paintings really are amazing."

"Now don't do that—don't you go sliding into the polite-conversation routine. No, no," she says before I can protest. "I'm sure you mean it. Hell, the paintings are wonderful. But you're getting the flat-eyed look of a girl on her best behavior, and we can't have that. Not when I was getting to know the real you."

"Sorry," I say. "I swear I'm not fading away on you."

Because I genuinely like her, I don't tell her that she's wrong—she hasn't met the real Nikki Fairchild. She's met Social Nikki who, much like Malibu Barbie, comes with a complete set of accessories. In my case, it's not a bikini and a convertible.

Instead, I have the *Elizabeth Fairchild Guide for Social Gatherings*.

My mother's big on rules. She claims it's her Southern upbringing. In my weaker moments, I agree. Mostly, I just think she's a controlling bitch. Since the first time she took me for tea at the Mansion at Turtle Creek in Dallas at age three, I have had the rules drilled into my head. How to walk, how to talk, how to dress. What to eat, how much to drink, what kinds of jokes to tell.

I have it all down, every trick, every nuance, and I wear my practiced pageant smile like armor against the world. The result being that I don't think I could truly be myself at a party even if my life depended on it.

This, however, is not something Evelyn needs to know.

"Where exactly are you living?" she asks.

"Studio City. I'm sharing a condo with my best friend from high school."

"Straight down the 101 for work and then back home again. No wonder you've only seen concrete.

Didn't anyone tell you that you should have taken an apartment on the Westside?"

"Too pricey to go it alone," I admit, and I can tell that my admission surprises her. When I make the effort— like when I'm Social Nikki—I can't help but look like I come from money. Probably because I do. Come from it, that is. But that doesn't mean I brought it with me.

"How old are you?"

"Twenty-four."

Evelyn nods sagely, as if my age reveals some secret about me. "You'll be wanting a place of your own soon enough. You call me when you do and we'll find you someplace with a view. Not as good as this one, of course, but we can manage something better than a freeway on-ramp."

"It's not that bad, I promise."

"Of course it's not," she says in a tone that says the exact opposite. "As for views," she continues, gesturing toward the now-dark ocean and the sky that's starting to bloom with stars, "you're welcome to come back anytime and share mine."

"I might take you up on that," I admit. "I'd love to

bring a decent camera back here and take a shot or two."

"It's an open invitation. I'll provide the wine and you can provide the entertainment. A young woman loose in the city. Will it be a drama? A rom-com? Not a tragedy, I hope. I love a good cry as much as the next woman, but I like you. You need a happy ending."

I tense, but Evelyn doesn't know she's hit a nerve. That's why I moved to LA, after all. New life. New story. New Nikki.

I ramp up the Social Nikki smile and lift my champagne flute. "To happy endings. And to this amazing party. I think I've kept you from it long enough."

"Bullshit," she says. "I'm the one monopolizing you, and we both know it."

We slip back inside, the buzz of alcohol-fueled conversation replacing the soft calm of the ocean.

"The truth is, I'm a terrible hostess. I do what I want, talk to whoever I want, and if my guests feel slighted they can damn well deal with it."

I gape. I can almost hear my mother's cries of horror all the way from Dallas.

"Besides," she continues, "this party isn't supposed to be about me. I put together this little shindig to introduce Blaine and his art to the community. He's the one who should be doing the mingling, not me. I may be fucking him, but I'm not going to baby him."

Evelyn has completely destroyed my image of how a hostess for the not-to-be-missed social event of the weekend is supposed to behave, and I think I'm a little in love with her for that.

"I haven't met Blaine yet. That's him, right?" I point to a tall reed of a man. He is bald, but sports a red goatee. I'm pretty sure it's not his natural color. A small crowd hums around him, like bees drawing nectar from a flower. His outfit is certainly as bright as one.

"That's my little center of attention, all right," Evelyn says. "The man of the hour. Talented, isn't he?" Her hand sweeps out to indicate her massive living room. Every wall is covered with paintings. Except for a few benches, whatever furniture was once in the room has been removed and replaced with easels on which more paintings stand.

I suppose technically they are portraits. The models are nudes, but these aren't like anything you would see in a classical art book. There's something edgy about them. Something provocative and raw. I can tell that they are expertly conceived and carried out, and yet they disturb me, as if they reveal more about the person viewing the portrait than about the painter or the model.

As far as I can tell, I'm the only one with that reaction. Certainly the crowd around Blaine is glowing. I can hear the gushing praise from here.

"I picked a winner with that one," Evelyn says. "But let's see. Who do you want to meet? Rip Carrington and Lyle Tarpin? Those two are guaranteed drama, that's for damn sure, and your roommate will be jealous as hell if you chat them up."

"She will?"

Evelyn's brows arch up. "Rip and Lyle? They've been feuding for weeks." She narrows her eyes at me. "The fiasco about the new season of their sitcom? It's all over the Internet? You really don't know them?"

"Sorry," I say, feeling the need to apologize. "My school schedule was pretty intense. And I'm sure you can imagine what working for Carl is like."

Speaking of …

I glance around, but I don't see my boss anywhere.

"That is one serious gap in your education," Evelyn says. "Culture—and yes, pop culture counts—is just as important as—what did you say you studied?"

"I don't think I mentioned it. But I have a double major in electrical engineering and computer science."

"So you've got brains and beauty. See? That's something else we have in common. Gotta say, though, with an education like that, I don't see why you signed up to be Carl's secretary."

I laugh. "I'm not, I swear. Carl was looking for someone with tech experience to work with him on the business side of things, and I was looking for a job where I could learn the business side. Get my feet wet. I think he was a little hesitant to hire me at first—my skills definitely lean toward tech—but I convinced him I'm a fast learner."

She peers at me. "I smell ambition."

I lift a shoulder in a casual shrug. "It's Los Angeles. Isn't that what this town is all about?"

"Ha! Carl's lucky he's got you. It'll be interesting to see how long he keeps you. But let's see … who here would intrigue you …?"

She casts about the room, finally pointing to a fifty-something man holding court in a corner. "That's Charles Maynard," she says. "I've known Charlie for years. Intimidating as hell until you get to know him. But it's worth it. His clients are either celebrities with name recognition or power brokers with more money than God. Either way, he's got all the best stories."

"He's a lawyer?"

"With Bender, Twain & McGuire. Very prestigious firm."

"I know," I say, happy to show that I'm not entirely ignorant, despite not knowing Rip or Lyle. "One of my closest friends works for the firm. He started here but he's in their New York office now."

"Well, come on, then, Texas. I'll introduce you." We take one step in that direction, but then Evelyn stops me. Maynard has pulled out his phone, and is shouting instructions at someone. I catch a few well-placed curses and eye Evelyn sideways. She looks unconcerned "He's a pussycat at heart. Trust me, I've worked with him before. Back in my agenting days, we put together more celebrity biopic deals for our clients than I can count. And we fought to keep a few tell-alls off the screen, too." She shakes her head, as if reliving those glory days, then pats my arm. "Still, we'll wait 'til he calms down a bit. In the meantime, though …"

She trails off, and the corners of her mouth turn down in a frown as she scans the room again. "I don't think he's here yet, but—oh! Yes! Now *there's* someone you should meet. And if you want to talk views, the house he's building has one that makes my view look like, well, like yours." She points toward the entrance hall, but all I see are bobbing heads and haute couture. "He hardly ever accepts invitations, but we go way back," she says.

I still can't see who she's talking about, but then the crowd parts and I see the man in profile. Goose bumps rise on my arms, but I'm not cold. In fact, I'm suddenly very, very warm.

He's tall and so handsome that the word is almost an insult. But it's more than that. It's not his looks, it's his *presence*. He commands the room simply by being in it, and I realize that Evelyn and I aren't the only ones looking at him. The entire crowd has noticed his arrival. He must feel the weight of all those eyes, and yet the attention doesn't faze him at all. He smiles at the girl with the champagne, takes a glass, and begins to chat casually with a woman who approaches him, a simpering smile stretched across her face.

"Damn that girl," Evelyn says. "She never did bring me my vodka."

But I barely hear her. "Damien Stark," I say. My voice surprises me. It's little more than breath.

Evelyn's brows rise so high I notice the movement in my peripheral vision. "Well, how about that?" she says knowingly. "Looks like I guessed right."

"You did," I admit. "Mr. Stark is just the man I want to see."

I hope you enjoyed the excerpt! Grab your own copy of Release Me … or any of the books in the series now!

The Original Trilogy

Release Me

Claim Me

Complete Me

And Beyond…

Anchor Me

Lost With Me

Some rave reviews for J. Kenner's sizzling romances...

I just get sucked into these books and can not get enough of this series. They are so well written and as satisfying as each book is they leave you greedy for more. — Goodreads reviewer on *Wicked Torture*

A sizzling, intoxicating, sexy read!!!! J. Kenner had me devouring Wicked Dirty, the second installment of *Stark World Series* in one sitting. I loved everything about this book from the opening pages to the raw and vulnerable characters. With her sophisticated prose, Kenner created a love story that had the perfect blend of lust, passion, sexual tension, raw emotions and love. - Michelle, Four Chicks Flipping Pages

Wicked Dirty CLAIMED and CONSUMED every ounce of me from the very first page. Mind racing. Pulse pounding. Breaths bated. Feels flowing. Eyes wide in anticipation. Heart beating out of my chest. I felt the current of *Wicked Dirty* flow through me. I was DRUNK on this book that was my fine whiskey, so smooth and spectacular, and could not get enough of this *Wicked Dirty* drink. - Karen Bookalicious Babes Blog

"Sinfully sexy and full of heart. Kenner shines in this second chance, slow burn of a romance. Wicked Grind is the perfect book to kick off your summer."- *K. Bromberg, New York Times bestselling author (on Wicked Grind)*

"J. Kenner never disappoints~her books just get better and better." - *Mom's Guilty Pleasure (on Wicked Grind)*

"I don't think J. Kenner could write a bad story if she tried. … Wicked Grind is a great beginning to what I'm positive will be a very successful series. … The line forms here." *iScream Books (On Wicked Grind)*

"Scorching, sweet, and soul-searing, *Anchor Me* is the ultimate love story that stands the test of time and tribulation. THE TRUEST LOVE!" *Bookalicious Babes Blog (on Anchor Me)*

"J. Kenner has brought this couple to life and the character connection that I have to these two holds no bounds and that is testament to J.

Kenner's writing ability." *The Romance Cover (on Anchor Me)*

"J. Kenner writes an emotional and personal story line. ... The premise will captivate your imagination; the characters will break your heart; the romance continues to push the envelope." *The Reading Café (on Anchor Me)*

"Kenner may very well have cornered the market on sinfully attractive, dominant antiheroes and the women who swoon for them . . ." *Romantic Times*

"*Wanted* is another J. Kenner masterpiece . . . This was an intriguing look at self-discovery and forbidden love all wrapped into a neat little action-suspense package. There was plenty of sexual tension and eventually action. Evan was hot, hot, hot! Together, they were combustible. But can we expect anything less from J. Kenner?" *Reading Haven*

"*Wanted* by J. Kenner is the whole package! A toe-curling smokin' hot read, full of incredible characters and a brilliant storyline that you won't be able to get enough of. I can't wait for the next book in this series . . . I'm hooked!" *Flirty & Dirty Book Blog*

"J. Kenner's evocative writing thrillingly captures the power of physical attraction, the pull of long-ing, the universe-altering effect one person can have on another. . . . *Claim Me* has the emotional depth to back up the sex . . . Every scene is infused with both erotic tension, and the tension of wondering what lies beneath Damien's veneer – and how and when it will be revealed." *Heroes and Heartbreakers*

"*Claim Me* by J. Kenner is an erotic, sexy and exciting ride. The story between Damien and Nikki is amazing and written beautifully. The intimate and detailed sex scenes will leave you fanning your-self to cool down. With the writing style of Ms. Kenner you almost feel like you are there in the story riding along the emotional rollercoaster with Damien and Nikki." *Fresh Fiction*

"PERFECT for fans of *Fifty Shades of Grey* and *Bared to You*. *Release Me* is a powerful and erotic romance novel that is sure to make adult romance readers sweat, sigh and swoon." *Reading, Eating & Dreaming Blog*

"I will admit, I am in the 'I loved *Fifty Shades*' camp,

but after reading *Release Me*, Mr. Grey only scratches the surface compared to Damien Stark." *Cocktails and Books Blog*

"It is not often when a book is so amazingly well-written that I find it hard to even begin to accurately describe it . . . I recommend this book to everyone who is interested in a passionate love story." *Romancebookworm's Reviews*

"The story is one that will rank up with the *Fifty Shades* and Cross Fire trilogies." *Incubus Publishing Blog*

"The plot is complex, the characters engaging, and J. Kenner's passionate writing brings it all perfectly together." *Harlequin Junkie*

Also by J. Kenner

The Stark Saga Novels:

Only his passion could set her free…

Meet Damien Stark

The Original Trilogy

Release Me

Claim Me

Complete Me

And Beyond…

Anchor Me

Lost With Me

Stark Ever After

(Stark Saga novellas):

Happily ever after is just the beginning.

The passion between Damien & Nikki continues.

Take Me

Have Me

Play My Game

Seduce Me

Unwrap Me

Deepest Kiss

Entice Me

Hold Me

Please Me

The Steele Books/Stark International:

He was the only man who made her feel alive.

Say My Name

On My Knees

Under My Skin

Take My Dare (includes short story Steal My Heart)

Stark International Novellas:

Meet Jamie & Ryan-so hot it sizzles.

Tame Me

Tempt Me

S.I.N. Trilogy:

It was wrong for them to be together…

…but harder to stay apart.

Dirtiest Secret

Hottest Mess

Sweetest Taboo

Stand alone novels:

Most Wanted:

Three powerful, dangerous men.

Three sensual, seductive women.

Wanted

Heated

Ignited

Wicked Nights (Stark World):

Sometimes it feels so damn good to be bad.

Wicked Grind

Wicked Dirty

Wicked Torture

Man of the Month

Who's your man of the month …?

Down On Me

Hold On Tight

Need You Now

Start Me Up

Get It On

In Your Eyes

Turn Me On

Shake It Up

All Night Long

In Too Deep

Light My Fire

Walk The Line

Bar Bites: A Man of the Month Cookbook(by J. Kenner & Suzanne M. Johnson)

Additional Titles

Wild Thing

One Night (A Stark World short story in the Second Chances anthology)

Also by Julie Kenner

The Protector (Superhero) Series:

The Cat's Fancy (prequel)

Aphrodite's Kiss

Aphrodite's Passion

Aphrodite's Secret

Aphrodite's Flame

Aphrodite's Embrace (novella)

Aphrodite's Delight (novella – free download)

Demon Hunting Soccer Mom Series:

Carpe Demon

California Demon

Demons Are Forever

Deja Demon

The Demon You Know (short story)

Demon Ex Machina

Pax Demonica

Day of the Demon

The Dark Pleasures Series:

Caress of Darkness

Find Me In Darkness

Find Me In Pleasure

Find Me In Passion

Caress of Pleasure

The Blood Lily Chronicles:

Tainted

Torn

Turned

Rising Storm:

Rising Storm: Tempest Rising

Rising Storm: Quiet Storm

Devil May Care:

Seducing Sin

Tempting Fate

About the Author

J. Kenner (aka Julie Kenner) is the *New York Times*, *USA Today*, *Publishers Weekly*, *Wall Street Journal* and #1 International bestselling author of over one hundred novels, novellas and short stories in a variety of genres.

JK has been praised by *Publishers Weekly* as an author with a "flair for dialogue and eccentric characterizations" and by *RT Bookclub* for having "cornered the market on sinfully attractive, dominant antiheroes and the women who swoon for them." A six-time finalist for Romance Writers of America's prestigious RITA award, JK took home the first RITA trophy awarded in the category of erotic romance in 2014 for her novel, *Claim Me* (book 2 of her Stark Trilogy).

In her previous career as an attorney, JK worked as a lawyer in Southern California and Texas. She currently lives in Central Texas, with her husband, two daughters, and two rather spastic cats.

More ways to connect:
www.jkenner.com
Text JKenner to 21000 for JK's text alerts.

facebook.com/jkennerbooks

twitter.com/juliekenner

79909114R00128

Made in the USA
Middletown, DE
13 July 2018